Granite Publishing Presents

Love Notes

#6

Savannah Nights

Savannah Nights

By Marnie L. Pehrson

~ ✧ ~

Savannah Nights

First edition January 2008

Published by:

Granite Publishing and Distribution, LLC
868 North 1430 West • Orem, Utah 84057
(801) 229-9023 • Toll Free (800) 574-5779
Fax (801) 229-1924
www.granitepublishing.biz

Cover Design by: Tammie Ingram
Page Layout and Design by: Myrna Varga, The Office Connection Inc.

ISBN: 978-1-59936-025-6
Library of Congress Control Number: 2008920021

10 9 8 7 6 5 4 3 2 1
Printed in the United States of America

Prologue

~ ✧ ~

Samantha Reynolds finished brushing her hair and crossed to her open bedroom window just in time to see Sean Cooper step out of his car. She caught a whiff of magnolia blossoms on the breeze and a melancholy ache tormented her heart. This would be her last night in Savannah—her last evening with her best friend.

The melancholy transformed into a flutter of anticipation. She and Sean had been inseparable through high school, and here they were the night before they would leave to pursue their education at separate universities. The tension between them had been mounting for months—a friendship that threatened to transform into something deeper. But they were out of time, and they both knew it.

Samantha moved to the side of the window and discreetly watched Sean saunter to the door, his lanky legs making the trip in no time at all. He was so cute, she could hardly imagine life without him. Perhaps these feelings were only on her end? Then again, Sean seemed to be experiencing them too. Even her mother remarked that she'd seen Sean gazing at Samantha with a love-struck look in his eyes.

Would they tell each other how they really felt tonight?

Would he finally kiss her? And if he did, was it all too little too late? Sean was off to UGA with a basketball scholarship and plans for becoming a lawyer. Samantha would leave for the Art Institute of Atlanta in the morning. Her thoughts drifted to her dreams of France and becoming a world-class chef. She knew she needed to pursue her dreams or she'd always regret it. But would she regret not telling Sean how she felt even more?

"Sam, Sean's here!" her brother Travis' voice called up the stairs.

Samantha grabbed her purse from the bed, gave her reflection a glance in the mirror and opened her bedroom door. Normally she would have trotted down the stairs, given Sean a hug and fairly jogged to the car. But not tonight, Sean asked her to dress up for dinner at the Pink House in historic Savannah.

Samantha wore a black tea-length dress with matching heels. It felt more like prom than a typical evening with Sean. Any other night they would have played basketball or gone to the movies. Her new shoes felt strange on her feet as she descended the stairs. She hoped that she wouldn't do something klutzy like trip and fall flat on her face.

About halfway down, Sean turned from his conversation with Travis, and his eyes caught Samantha's. He put a hand to his heart with a dramatic flair, "Sam! You're gorgeous!"

Samantha hoped her cheeks weren't as crimson as they felt. She affected formality, "You look very handsome too, Mr. Cooper. Is that a new suit?" Sean shook his head and took her hand.

"Don't you two look adorable!" Marjorie Reynolds exclaimed

and lifted her camera to her face. "Just a couple of pictures before you leave."

Sean put his arm around Samantha's shoulder and she slipped hers around his waist. Marjorie snapped one picture, then another and another.

"Mom, that's enough," Samantha pleaded, blinking away the flash spots from her vision.

"Well, this is a momentous occasion. You'll want to remember it," Marjorie reasoned. "Who knows when you two will get to see each other again?"

Samantha and Sean looked at each other with a somber expression. When would they see each other again? The seriousness of the moment seemed to sink in for both of them, then Marjorie's camera flash interrupted the moment.

Sean looked toward Samantha's mother, "We better get going. Our reservation's at six." He glanced at his watch.

Marjorie kissed each of them on the cheek and then stood at the door watching them walk to the car. Sean opened Samantha's door, and she waved back at her mother. Sean gave Marjorie one last wave while he crossed to the driver's side and slipped behind the wheel of his Honda Civic.

"Your mom's an angel," Sean observed as he backed out of the driveway.

"Well, maybe not an *angel*." *Do angels have manipulative streaks?* Samantha wondered.

"There aren't too many people in this world better than your mother," Sean's serious voice seemed almost to scold Samantha for her thoughts. He shifted the car into gear and pulled onto the street.

"Agreed," Samantha nodded, and Sean reached for her hand, lacing his fingers with hers. Over the last month or so, he'd been holding her hand every chance he got. The gesture made Sam wonder again if they would admit how they felt about each other tonight.

Instead they discussed UGA basketball all the way to the Pink House. Samantha was just as enthusiastic about the game as her friend, and she was absolutely thrilled that he would have the opportunity to play for the team. Sean had worked hard for his basketball scholarship. The star forward deserved this reward. Samantha's only regret was that she wouldn't be able to attend his games like she had in high school.

"Maybe you can come visit for some of the games," Sean suggested as they walked up the cobblestone streets toward the Pink House.

"That would be fun," Samantha gave his hand a squeeze. "I'll definitely watch the games on TV when they're on. Just imagine me screaming your name." She chuckled.

"I'll do that," his eyes met hers so intently that she half expected him to lean over and kiss her. But he didn't.

They strolled in silence, listening to the crickets and the traffic. They turned down another square and Sean broke the silence, "Have you ever been to the Pink House?"

"No, I think Mom has though," she replied.

"Well, you do remember the story behind it, don't you?" Sean asked. He seemed pleased when she shook her head that she didn't. "For one thing, they say it's haunted."

"Everything's haunted in Savannah, Sean. It's built on graves." Samantha stared up at the gnarled live oak trees dripping with Spanish moss. While her comment had been sarcastic, the trees seemed to attest to its veracity.

Sean chuckled and continued. "Seriously, I have a cousin who worked as a busboy here. He said it's definitely haunted. Seems the man who originally commissioned the construction of this home didn't like that it turned out pink; it was originally red brick, but he didn't like that. They put white stucco over the top, but the red brick bled through and turned the house pink. The man wanted to tear it down, but his wife liked it. In fact she liked it so much that she ran off with the architect."

"Poor guy," Samantha shook her head.

"It gets worse. The husband was so grief-stricken that he committed suicide. My cousin says he's seen him peeping through the kitchen service window and dishes mysteriously move around the place.

Samantha looked into Sean's face trying to determine if he really believed this tale. "You're serious. You really believe that?"

Sean shrugged, "Strange things happen in Savannah, Sam. It's part of its charm. Part of what I love about it."

"Well, it sells tour tickets and bed and breakfast stays, but a lot of it sounds a bit farfetched to me," Samantha reasoned.

"Maybe, but my cousin Jeff swears he's seen things move around the Pink House and bearded ghosts staring at him through windows."

"Is Jeff the one who had five imaginary friends when he was

little?" Samantha teased. "I believe their names were Big Donnie, Little Donnie, Poonoo, Dr. Toebooger, and what was the other one?" Samantha started laughing.

Sean rolled his eyes, released her hand and put his arm around her shoulder, tugging her toward the restaurant, "That was Beth, not Jeff."

"Oh, okay," Samantha chuckled. "Just wanted to double check."

They entered the restaurant and the waiter took them to their table. Once seated, Samantha couldn't help looking around the place, half-expecting to see a disembodied torso float by their table or hover in a window. As much as she liked to tease Sean about his belief in old Savannah legends, she secretly hoped they were true. She left the door of her mind cracked for the possibility.

Her eyes fixed on a portrait over the fireplace, "You reckon that's the man who haunts this place?"

Sean looked over his shoulder at the portrait. "Must be."

Samantha ran her hand along the white tablecloth. "So fancy." She gestured to her wine glass filled with water and adjusted the silverware next to the china plate. "I can't wait to have a restaurant like this someday."

"A haunted one?" Sean teased.

"Yeah—right. No, an upscale one in Atlanta or maybe even a café in France."

~ ✧ ~

Sean took a deep breath and rubbed his perspiring palm against his suit pants. He'd been crazy about Samantha since ninth grade. She'd come up to him in gym class and introduced herself. He was the new kid in town while Samantha had grown up with everyone and had tons of friends. When she learned they lived in the same neighborhood, she befriended him, introduced him to her friends, and made him feel welcome.

He even credited Sam for the fact that he got playing time on the JV basketball team his freshman year. Coach Crisman was a friend of her family, and Sam personally introduced Sean to the coach, raving about what a great player he was. Her inside knowledge of Sean's basketball skills had come from playing horse in her driveway—hardly enough to be credible. But for whatever reason, Coach Crisman heeded Samantha's counsel and played Sean when most coaches would have ignored the new kid on the block in favor of the boys who'd grown up in the local leagues.

Sean's thoughts came back to the present. He couldn't stop staring at Sam with her blonde hair resting softly on her shoulders. She looked incredible in that dress, and her eyes were even greener tonight.

He wanted to reach across the table, take Samantha's hand, and declare his love for her. He'd say he couldn't bear to be apart from her. Then he'd beg her to come to UGA with him.

"You'll come to my restaurant, won't you?" she was saying. "You'll tip my waiters generously when you're a big time lawyer, right?"

Sean had rehearsed the conversation in his mind a dozen times. But as he listened to her talk about different aspects of the Pink House restaurant, comparing it to the one she would someday run, he couldn't bring himself to say the words. He couldn't ask her to sacrifice her dream for him.

"Sure, I'll spend lots of money at your restaurant," he replied instead.

~ ✧ ~

The sun had set, but the Savannah streets were lit by lamps and houselights from the refurbished mansions on the squares. Samantha and Sean had ambled a couple of blocks from the Pink House enjoying the beautiful historic atmosphere. Suddenly, Samantha stopped and announced, "I'm sorry, Sean, I just can't do this anymore." An apprehensive expression came over Sean's face.

Samantha reached down and unfastened the strap on her shoe. "I cannot walk another step in these heels on these cobblestone streets." She pulled off one shoe and then the other and let the pair dangle from her finger by the straps.

"Well then," Sean sighed and then chuckled, "I'll just have to carry you the rest of the way." He swept her up in his arms and started down the street with her.

"Sean!" she slapped his shoulder. "Put me down. I can walk."

"I can't let you traipse barefoot around Savannah. What kind of gentleman would I be?" He tightened his grip on her.

Samantha fluttered her bare feet, "It's ninety degrees out here. There's no way my feet are going to get cold."

"We wouldn't want you to make a scene going barefoot in front of all these tourists. They'll go back up North claiming southerners don't wear shoes."

Two people stared at them as they passed. "I think we're making more of a scene this way," Samantha observed.

He didn't reply, just carried her to the end of the square.

"Come on, Sean, I weigh a ton. I'm going to break your back," she reasoned.

"You're light. Besides, I'm on an athletic scholarship. Remember?"

"For basketball, not weightlifting," she retorted. He refused to heed her warning and sauntered on. Samantha relented and stared up at the Spanish moss dangling from gnarled limbs. The stars blinked from beyond the trees and she wondered why she was protesting. If she were smart, she'd remember this moment and file it away as the most romantic of her life.

She told her mind to press the record button and save this memory for replay when she was alone at culinary school. When she looked into Sean's face again, he was gazing at her the way she knew she must be looking at him—with a longing desire to never be separated.

He stopped walking and his face drew closer to hers, his lips hovering less than an inch from Samantha's. Her heart pounded and her mouth watered. Samantha let her hand rest on Sean's cheek and would have pulled his lips the rest of the way to her own, but a man slapped Sean on the shoulder, "Hey, can you two kids tell me which way Nathaniel Green Square is?"

Sean closed his eyes, and released a sigh as if he'd been holding a deep breath. He let Samantha down, and she felt her bare feet touch the warm cobblestone.

Sean pointed, "Go left over here at the next street, walk a couple blocks and it's the only square that doesn't have Spanish moss on the trees."

Samantha smiled up at Sean, "Yeah, in life Nathaniel Green hated Spanish moss so much that it won't grow on his square."

"Thanks," the man said.

"I see you've been listening to my history lessons after all." Sean started to lift her again, but Samantha put her hand on his chest.

"It's okay, Sean, really. I can walk."

Sean rubbed his back a little. "Okay, if you insist," he chuckled.

~ ✧ ~

After a romantic stroll along the river, Sean took Sam home. They sat on her front porch talking and laughing. It was a little past midnight when Sean stood to leave. He accompanied Samantha to the door and she turned to face him.

Sean hugged her.

"I sure am going to miss you, Sean," she said.

"Me too," he whispered. Sean's heart hammered as he leaned to give her a quick kiss goodbye. He never could bring himself to say the words that were in his heart, but he couldn't let her leave without giving her some indication of how he felt.

At that instant, he decided he wanted to really kiss her—not some faint peck on the lips, but a real kiss. After all, she was the only girl he'd ever loved. Sean held her face in his hands and kissed her again. Samantha responded immediately, and he knew that she felt more for him than friendship. He held her tight, memorizing how she felt in his arms and the strawberry scent of her hair. He kissed her again and allowed himself to express with his lips what he could never say with words—that there had never been nor ever could be anyone else for him but her.

After some time, Sean finally pulled her against him and whispered into her ear, "Why haven't we ever done this before?" He hoped she would say something—anything to indicate that she wanted to be with him as much as he wanted to be with her.

But Samantha just shrugged—her green eyes moist and staring up into his. Sean's heart sank and he knew she wouldn't change her plans for him, and he couldn't ask her to. He leaned over and kissed her lightly, hugged her and whispered into her ear, "Write me." He turned toward his car and never looked back.

Chapter 1

~ ✧ ~

Over 10 years later . . .

Samantha Reynolds felt her mother's arm slip around her shoulder and give her a squeeze. "I'm so glad you were able to come for Christmas this year, Sam."

"Me too, I thought for sure I'd get stuck working," Samantha smiled as she stood at her mother's kitchen counter peeling potatoes.

"Make a few more," Marjorie said. "There'll be an extra guest tonight."

"Really?" Sam looked at her mother. "Who?"

"It's a surprise," Marjorie winked and went to the stove to stir her pot of chicken and dumplings.

"Oh Mom, you're not trying to set me up with one of those guys from your office again, are you?" Samantha's shoulders slumped a little with her sigh.

Marjorie only answered with a mischievous wink. Just then the doorbell rang. "I'll get that," Marjorie said and left the kitchen.

While Samantha continued peeling potatoes, she wondered what her mother had up her sleeve this time. She was always trying to set her up with men. Sam knew it had everything to do with Marjorie wanting more grandchildren. But what was the point in arranging meetings with men in Savannah when Samantha lived in Atlanta? Probably all part of her mother's plan to get her to move back home.

Samantha thought once her brother's wife had given birth to their little boy her Mom would leave her alone, but it hadn't worked. She still constantly called, wanting to know if there was anyone special in Samantha's life. Of course there wasn't—not since Jerry. The mere thought of Jerry made Samantha frown.

"Look who's here, Sam!" Marjorie exclaimed as she entered the kitchen carrying little Tyson on her hip.

Samantha turned her head and the sight of her nephew made a smile spread across her face. She crossed the kitchen, wiping her hands on her apron.

"Oh, isn't he adorable!" she exclaimed. Just behind her mother was her sister-in-law Leslie. "Hi Leslie!" she greeted, then gave Tyson's chubby cheeks a light pinch and a kiss. She hugged Leslie next, and by the time they had exchanged pleasantries, Travis had entered the kitchen. He gave his sister a big hug and asked her about work.

"It's going well, thanks," Samantha answered. "What about you?"

"Staying busy," Travis replied and took his son from Marjorie. "I'll keep Tyson out of your hair so you ladies can chat."

"Yeah, yeah," Leslie teased, and moved an auburn lock from her eyes. "You're just trying to get out of helping in the kitchen." She gave her tall husband's arm a little punch.

"You've got that right!" he nodded as he carried the baby into the living room and sat down on the couch. He reached over and flipped on the television.

Marjorie stepped out of the kitchen. "I'll go get Tyson a few toys," she announced as she headed toward the stairs.

Leslie followed Samantha back to the counter and helped her cut potatoes.

"So, who is Mom's mystery guest tonight?" Samantha probed, hoping Leslie might know what her mother was up to.

"What guest?" Leslie asked.

"Mom says she's invited someone to dinner tonight—a surprise guest."

"Maybe she's got a date," Leslie suggested. "Travis and I think she might be dating someone."

"Oh?" Samantha's eyes caught Leslie's.

"Yeah, she's pretty secretive about it. Maybe you can get it out of her," Leslie suggested.

"Or maybe if I don't bug her, she won't bug me!" Samantha countered.

Her sister-in-law smiled at her. "Is she giving you a hard time again?"

"Always," Samantha rolled her green eyes. "I really thought she'd lighten up after Tyson was born, but she almost seems worse than ever."

"She just wants you to be happy. She worries that you're lonely." Leslie dropped a handful of chopped potatoes into a pot.

Samantha carried the pot to the sink and filled it with water. "I suppose so, but the pressure makes it worse." Samantha carried the potatoes to the stove and turned on the heat.

In a few minutes, Marjorie returned. The three women continued to work in the kitchen together and talk. Just as the final items were placed in the oven to cook, the doorbell rang. Instead of answering it, Marjorie stepped toward Samantha. She wiped some flour from Samantha's cheek with a dishtowel and removed the scrunchie from Samantha's hair. She fluffed her daughter's blond locks and adjusted them on her shoulders.

"Mom," Samantha pleaded. "You didn't. You're setting me up with some blind date again, aren't you?"

"I assure you, he's not blind," Marjorie winked and called toward the other room. "Travis, will you please get that?"

Travis left the baby playing on the floor by the couch and went to the door. Marjorie untied Samantha's apron and removed it.

Samantha's pleading gaze begged Leslie for help, but her sister-in-law just covered her mouth to keep from laughing. Samantha sighed and her mother motioned for her to follow her.

Reluctantly, Samantha stepped into the living room. Her jaw dropped when her eyes met her mother's guest. He was hugging Travis by the door.

Samantha didn't even think, just hurried toward the man. "Sean! How have you been? It's been ages!" she exclaimed as she hugged him.

Her old friend gathered her in his arms and gave her a tight squeeze. Then he released her and held her at arms length, "Sam, you're gorgeous!"

Samantha blushed a little and looked up into his face. Sean Cooper was hardly the lanky basketball player she'd known in high school. He'd filled out, but he had the same thick black hair and penetrating blue eyes he always did. And there was that smile she'd been so fond of.

"Well, you don't look half bad yourself!" she said. Her eyes shifted from his handsome face down to his white Oxford, forest green sweater and jeans. He looked wonderful, she thought as her eyes met his blue ones once more. "I wish Mom had told me you were coming, I would have hunted the old photo albums," Samantha gave her mother a glance. *And I would have taken more pains with my appearance*, she thought. For once, one of her mother's surprise visitors was someone Samantha wanted to see.

"How long has it been?" Sean asked, his hands still on her shoulders.

"Ten years, at least," Samantha shook her head.

She took him by the hand and led him over to the couch. "Have a seat and tell me what you've been up to."

They sat down next to each other and within moments, Marjorie had produced an old photo album. "Here you go. I found this in Samantha's room. I thought you two would enjoy looking through it together."

Leslie picked up Tyson and shifted him on her hip. She tugged her husband's shirt sleeve and motioned for him to follow her back to the kitchen. When he started to sit down and join in the conversation with Sean and Samantha, Marjorie grabbed his other arm and the two women fairly dragged their reluctant prisoner to the kitchen.

"Mom tells me you're a city alderman now," Samantha said as she sat sideways, one leg tucked under her so she could face her friend.

Sean nodded, "And you're a famous chef in Atlanta."

Samantha rolled her eyes. "Hardly famous."

"I've read the reviews in the *Atlanta Constitution*. You're famous there at least."

Samantha shook her head, still denying the compliment. "So have you and Ellen set a date for the wedding yet?" Samantha asked.

"No, we broke up," Sean confided.

Samantha tried to hide her elation with an "I'm sorry to hear that."

"Don't be," he responded. "It just wouldn't have worked."

Samantha couldn't have agreed more. She'd never met the woman, but her mother told her a little. Hard, driven, and pushy were the adjectives Marjorie had used. Ellen didn't sound like a good match for Sean. Then again, Samantha had to admit that she probably wouldn't see anyone as a good match for him—no one other than herself that is.

"I'm glad to have a break from women for a while. I need to focus on my work for a change." Sean said.

"A confirmed old bachelor," Samantha winked.

"Yeah, that sounds good to me," Sean agreed. "Women are just too much trouble." He looked up to see Marjorie standing in the doorway and added with a gesture toward her and then Samantha, "Present company excepted, of course."

"Of course," Marjorie nodded and returned to the kitchen.

Sean reached for the photo album on the coffee table. "Do we dare look through this?" he asked Samantha.

"Hey, you weren't the gangly tomboy. I'm the one who should dread looking through these photos, not you," she countered and scooted next to him on the couch. They held the album between them and went through the photos page by page, laughing and remembering episodes from their youth until Marjorie called them to dinner.

~ ✧ ~

As the evening ended, Samantha accompanied Sean to his car. "I'm so glad Mom thought to invite you. It was fun catching up on old times," she said.

"Those photos were hilarious—you with your braces and me with my acne," Sean laughed.

"And that crazy beard you tried to grow," Samantha added. "You looked like Shaggy hunting down Scooby snacks." Samantha chuckled and reached up to touch his chin. The stubble she felt there held no resemblance to the soft wispy hairs of his youth. The old attraction she'd felt for him their senior year was still there, only intensified by the man he'd become.

Sean put his hand on her wrist, then laced his fingers with hers. Samantha's pulse raced with the familiarity of the gesture. It had been over ten years since they'd stood on her mother's front porch and said their goodbyes, yet, it could have been yesterday from the way her insides fluttered at his touch.

"What happened to us?" Sean asked, his eyes meeting hers.

Samantha shrugged, "We grew up. We did what we set out to do."

"I mean that night . . . we didn't stay in touch like we said we would." His voice was husky, and Samantha could feel a lump forming in her throat. She knew the night he spoke of. It was burned in her memory, never to be forgotten.

"I guess we just got busy with our lives, our careers," Samantha shrugged.

"Yeah," Sean nodded. "We grew up. We're not those kids anymore, are we?"

"No, thank heavens," Samantha chuckled, thinking of how immature and awkward she'd been at seventeen and eighteen. She'd learned a lot about life since then.

Sean's face grew somber. "I guess it's all for the best. We're both happy with our lives the way they are—right?"

"Right," Samantha agreed, but a part of her knew she was lying.

Sean released her hand and retrieved his keys from his pocket. Samantha's stomach felt like a rock had plummeted to the bottom of it. He was leaving and who knew when she'd see him again.

"Well, kiddo, I guess I better get going. I've got an early morning." He leaned over and kissed her cheek. "Don't be such a stranger."

She forced a smile, "Yeah, we'll have to get together again before another ten years passes."

"Definitely," he agreed, and opened his car door.

"Take care of yourself, Sean," she said just before he closed his door. She pulled her coat tighter around her and watched him back out and drive away. His sudden change in demeanor told her all she needed to know. He realized, just as she did, that they were both committed to their careers—careers in cities four hours apart. A long distance relationship now wouldn't work any better than it had before.

Chapter 2

~ ✧ ~

Three days later . . .

"Are you sure you don't want to call Sean before you leave and tell him goodbye?" Marjorie prompted as she carried a big gift bag of presents out to Samantha's car.

"I'm sure, Mom. If he wanted to see me again, he would have called."

"We are in the twenty-first century now, Sam. A woman can be the one to make the first call," Marjorie insisted.

Sam opened the trunk and put her suitcase in while Marjorie put the bag in beside it.

"Is that what you do? Call men up for dates?" Samantha chuckled. She remembered Leslie's comment about her mother seeing someone. Sam never had gotten around to asking her about that. Marjorie frequently dated, that wasn't anything new. If there had been anyone serious, her mother would have said something.

Marjorie shook her head in frustration. "Never mind honey, it's your life. I'll stop meddling."

Samantha put a hand on her mother's arm, "I'm sorry I've been such a grump, Mom. I really do appreciate you asking Sean to dinner. It was wonderful seeing him again."

"I'm glad. And I'm sorry I've been so pushy. I know you need your space. I just worry about you." Marjorie put her hand to her daughter's cheek. "You do know I love you, don't you?"

"Of course I do, Mom. I love you too."

Marjorie hugged Samantha tight and whispered in her ear, "Just remember if there's anyone you can trust, it's Sean Cooper."

"I know, Mom." Samantha agreed. "It's just not going to work out with us. The timing's never right. Besides, I really don't think he's interested."

Marjorie put her hands on Sam's shoulders. Her expression grew earnest and she seemed to be struggling for the right words, "But, you'd lean on Sean if anything happened to me, wouldn't you? Sean would be there for you if you needed him."

"You're worrying me, Mom. What's going on?" Samantha searched her mother's grave expression.

"It's nothing." Marjorie shrugged and lightened her expression. "I've just had some stresses at work is all, and I keep thinking if I'm not around to tie up loose ends, Sean would know how. Besides, he could be there for you so you wouldn't be lonely."

"What do you think is going to happen to you?" Samantha pressed.

"Oh, nothing," Marjorie slapped her hand at the air. "Don't worry about it. I stress too much about work. I'll be around for years and years. You'll probably be sick of me at your house, spoiling your kids," her mom said with a grin. "Of course, you'll have to actually *date* someone if you hope to get married," she added with a wink.

"Mom," Sam rolled her eyes, exasperation edging her voice. "When I'm ready, it will happen."

"Don't wait too long, dear," her mother advised. "You never know what tomorrow will bring."

~ ✧ ~

Samantha spent the evening driving from Savannah to Atlanta. She opened her apartment door, let down her blonde hair from its ponytail and tossed her keys on the kitchen table. Stretching her hands high above her head with a yawn, she crossed to the window. Samantha opened the drapes and looked out at the cold gray evening. She wished she could have stayed in Savannah a little longer, but she had to work the next day.

Samantha sighed as her fingers picked at the wilted needles on her miniature Christmas tree. The after-Christmas blahs were settling in already. The cryptic statement her mother made earlier that day didn't help matters either. Her words kept running though Samantha's mind like a haunting refrain.

"If anything happens to me . . . Sean would know how to tie up lose ends." Her mother had tossed the statement out like a mysterious unmatched sock one finds in her dryer.

How would Sean be able to help if something did happen to her mother? What was going on at work that made her this worried? It gave Samantha an eerie feeling of foreboding. Maybe she should call her. She reached for the phone, but then decided against it. Her mom was probably still trying to play match-maker between Sam and Sean. This cryptic statement was just her way of dropping a mysterious lure out there in hopes that Sam would take the bait and call Sean to find out what was going on.

Marjorie had always hoped that Samantha and Sean would end up together. Even Samantha had to admit she still had feelings for Sean, but the timing had never been right. Now she lived in Atlanta, and he was in Savannah. She thought of the evening she'd just spent with him and smiled. It was as if the ten years they'd spent apart had never happened. They had picked up exactly where they left off. But then Sam remembered their parting and the smile fled. She and Sean were a nice idea, but not a practical one. It was never going to happen.

Samantha opened the freezer and pulled out a frozen dinner. She only kept them on hand for emergency situations—evenings like this when she was just too exhausted to slave over a stove. Being head chef at the Chart House in Atlanta kept Samantha cooking enough. Still she enjoyed preparing meals at home as well—but not tonight.

She popped the dinner in the microwave and turned on the television. She decided she'd get her mind off things by watching a movie. Samantha inserted a DVD and sat down on the couch to eat her meal. Before the movie was halfway through, she fell asleep.

Sirens wailed, waking Samantha from her slumber. She sat up and yawned, stretching her long arms high above her head. Standing up, she peeked out the window to see flashing lights speeding down the road. The police cars whizzed by, and Samantha picked up the remote to turn on the news.

She sat back down and stared blankly at the television, unable to focus her attention. Her mind wandered back to her mother and her comments to her earlier that afternoon. Samantha looked at the clock. It was eleven thirty, too late to be making phone calls, but she couldn't shake the feeling that she should call her mother. She reached for her portable phone on the table next to the couch and hit the talk button. Her mother wouldn't mind. The phone rang and rang. Sam's eyebrows knit together.

"Where would she be at this late hour?" she mumbled. At last, someone picked up.

"Hello, Mom?" she said. There was no reply. "Mom, are you there?" Samantha heard a heavy exhale, as if someone had been holding their breath.

"Samantha," the voice whispered, then all fell silent.

"Mom!" Samantha screamed. "Mom!"

No reply.

Samantha hung up the phone and tried to call the number again, but now it was busy. Her fingers frantically dialed her brother's number.

She stood up when she heard Travis answer the phone. "Travis, I think there's something wrong with Mom. Will you run by her house and check on her?"

"I'm sure she's fine. I just talked to her a few hours ago." Travis yawned. "But I'll stop by there in the morning on my way to work."

"No, do it now! I just called over there, and she sounded really odd. She just said my name, and then didn't say anything else. When I tried to call back, it was busy."

"Maybe you caught her in a phone call, and she just switched over for a minute and lost you," her brother suggested.

"No, Travis. Something's wrong. Just go by there . . . please!" Samantha pleaded.

"All right, all right," Travis assured in a calming voice. "I'll get dressed and go over there."

"Thanks!" Samantha disconnected the call and paced the floor. She periodically tried to call her mother again, with no success.

Chapter 3

~ ✧ ~

Three days later . . .

Travis held a black umbrella over Samantha's head and slipped his arm around her shoulder. She shuddered from the bone-chilling cold that came less from the drizzling rain and more from the hollow pain that needled her heart. Travis pulled her close and together they watched the pallbearers lower their mother's casket into the grave. The minister offered a few final words, but Samantha did not register them. Her mind was too preoccupied with questions. How could her youthful mother be here—in this cold lonely place?

It had happened so suddenly that Samantha could hardly process it all. The phone call three days earlier hadn't seemed real. When she'd heard Travis' voice telling her that their mother was gone, Samantha shook her head in confusion. "Gone where?" She'd just seen her. When Travis stopped by their mother's to check on her, he'd found her dead in her bed upstairs with the portable phone on the floor beside her. He called an ambulance, but it was too late. Marjorie Reynolds was already gone.

"At least she didn't suffer," Travis tried to cushion the blow.

"The doctor said she went fast. It looks like she had a heart attack."

Samantha was glad her mother hadn't suffered long, but still it gave her little consolation. For the longest time she couldn't believe what Travis had told her. She wasn't even aware of her mother having a heart problem.

She watched her brother's gloved hand grip the clod of earth and release it. Mechanically she followed his lead and did the same. With the sound of dirt pelting the oak casket, the chilly December air settled deeper inside Samantha—into the sinewy muscle of her heart, into her blood and coursed through her veins, until it completely filled her with a frosty void.

When her brother turned and suggested they leave, she followed him and then stopped. A man in an overcoat stood before her. It was Sean, his eyes misty. He shook Travis' hand and offered his condolences. When Sean's attention returned to Samantha, Travis continued on. Taking his wife's arm, he left Samantha alone with her friend.

"I'm so sorry, Sam." He put out his arms and she fell against him, crying tears against his coat. "You know how much I loved Marjorie," he whispered into her hair.

"I know, Sean. She loved you too." A flood of memories returned. She thought of the afternoons she spent shooting baskets with Sean and Travis outside their house. She could almost hear her mother's voice calling them in for pizza. They'd crowd around the kitchen table, laugh and act silly. Marjorie would join in like she was one of them.

"I just can't believe she's gone," he held her tighter against him.

"Me either. It feels like a nightmare," she cried. Surely she should be able to pinch herself and awaken from this horrible dream. But it wasn't a dream. It was one of those times when even one's worst nightmare is preferable to reality.

"It just doesn't make any sense," Sean whispered.

He was right. It didn't make any sense, but the autopsy clearly indicated a heart attack. There was no other explanation. Sean accompanied Samantha to her car. She unlocked it and he stood outside her door while she slid behind the wheel.

"Are you sure you feel up to driving," he asked. "I'd be happy to drive you wherever you want to go."

"That's okay," she said, shaking her head. "I can manage. I'm just going back to Mom's for a while."

"Are you sure you should go there?" His eyes narrowed a little. "There are so many memories . . ."

"It's where I want to be right now. I just need some time alone to sort things out." She looked up into his concerned eyes.

He put a hand on her shoulder, leaned over and kissed her cheek. "Call me if you need anything," he said.

"I will . . . thanks, Sean."

He shut the door and stood there watching as she started the engine and drove away.

~ ✧ ~

Samantha sat on her mother's flower print sofa, her eyes fixed blankly on the Christmas tree lights. She pulled the burgundy afghan tighter over her shoulders and shoved her chin beneath it. Her hands rubbed her arms, attempting to warm the chill that wouldn't leave her.

Samantha brushed a tear from her cheek as she continued to study the Christmas tree. Had it only been last week that she and Travis' family had gathered around the tree with Mom and sang Christmas carols? They'd listened to Travis read the Christmas story and kept with their long-standing Christmas Eve tradition of opening one present each.

Marjorie Reynolds was young—only fifty. To Samantha, she felt more like her friend than her mother. In fact, Marjorie looked so young and dressed so stylishly that when she and Samantha went out for lunch, the waiters sometimes mistook them for sisters, even though there was twenty-two years difference in their ages.

Samantha thought back on all the things her mother had taught her, all the happy memories. Having no father to help raise them, Marjorie taught her children everything they needed to know. She schooled them in fixing leaky drains, patching drywall, baking bread and doing laundry. Marjorie worked hard as a legal secretary over the years for a prestigious law firm in Savannah, Georgia. She'd saved enough to send Samantha to culinary school in Atlanta, then Travis started at UGA two years later.

While Marjorie's savings covered tuition, both siblings still had to work to cover other expenses. Nothing had ever come easily for the small family, but Marjorie's "trudge on and make the best of it" philosophy carried them through. Samantha hadn't realized how much she'd leaned on her mother's steadiness and determination until now. Samantha felt suddenly she was flying without a net. There was no one to catch her when she fell, no one to comfort her when things went awry.

It wasn't that Samantha hadn't learned to fend for herself. She'd been forced to learn self-preservation as the daughter of a hard-working single mother, and she'd been on her own in Atlanta since her days at the culinary institute. But still, Mom had always been there to run to, to pick up the phone and call. She comforted Samantha through every heartbreak and challenge—from listening to her rant when her high school basketball team lost the state championship to picking up the pieces of Samantha's shattered heart when her fiancé broke off their engagement a week before the wedding.

The loneliness settled upon Samantha like a cold rain that seeped into every cell of her body. Sure, she had Travis. But Travis had a busy career and his own wife and son to think about. He didn't have time to mollycoddle his older sister.

Samantha suddenly rose to her feet and went to the kitchen in search of hot chocolate. As she heated the mug of water in the microwave, she realized that it was her turn to step up to the plate and take her mother's place, to be the glue that held the little family together.

She'd start off in the morning by being the brave one to go through their mother's things. She'd take care of closing up the house until they could decide what to do with it.

Samantha carried her hot chocolate up the stairs, stirring it the whole way. She brushed back the stray strand of blonde hair that fell on her face, then opened the door to her old bedroom. She flipped on the light. The room looked just the way it did ten years ago when she left for college. Her toy basketball goal still hung from the door. Her basketball trophies and collection of carousel horses still lined the bookshelf on the far wall. Samantha knew that her mother had kept her room in its last inhabited condition, but seeing it again this evening made her feel it would be incredibly wrong to go through her mother's things. Perhaps she and Travis should let the house stand as it was—as a memorial to the mother who loved them. Marjorie Reynolds had done no less for them.

She set her hot chocolate on the doily atop her bedside table and looked around the room, running her hands through her hair. In a flash of resolution, her green eyes sparked. She lifted the receiver on the phone by the bed and dialed her brother's number.

"Travis, did I wake you?" she asked.

"No, it's all right. What's up?" Travis asked.

"I have an idea." She could hear the excitement in her own voice.

"What's that?"

She rushed on, "You know how Mom left our bedrooms the way they were before we left for college. She said it made her feel close to us when we were away."

"Yeah . . ." There was a hint of caution in Travis' voice.

"Maybe we should leave her house this way . . . the way she lived in it. Then all we have to do is come here to feel close to her."

"Uh . . ." Travis hesitated. "It's a nice sentiment."

"So you think it's a good idea?" Samantha asked.

"Actually, I was going to say that it's a nice sentiment, but it's not practical," he clarified.

"Why not?"

"Because we can't keep paying property taxes and insurance on a house that nobody lives in," he reasoned.

"Why not? We both have good jobs. If we went in on it together—?"

"Sam," Travis interrupted her. "I know you miss Mom, but keeping her house isn't going to let us keep her."

"But don't you think it seems wrong somehow . . . to rummage through her things and divide them up . . . " Sam's voice cracked. "Or trash them when she spent the last ten years keeping our rooms like memorial shrines to our youth?"

"This isn't the same, Sam. Mom would understand. She wouldn't expect us to keep the house as a shrine to her."

Samantha's shoulders slumped as she released a hopeless sigh. She knew her brother was right, but it just seemed wrong somehow. Something had to remain as a memorial to Marjorie Reynolds—something more lasting than Samantha's recollections, which would eventually dim with time.

"Get some sleep, Sam. It sounds like you need it," Travis advised.

Samantha sighed, "I'll try."

"Night, Sam."

"See ya."

Samantha set down the phone and pulled back the bedding. She hadn't gotten any sleep at Travis' house the night before. She couldn't see why tonight, in this house full of memories, would be any different.

~ ✧ ~

Samantha slept better than she imagined she would in her

old bedroom and when the sun's early morning rays streamed in through the bedroom window, she felt refreshed. She opened her eyes and lay there, staring out the window at the sunny winter morning. She settled her hands behind her head and lay there in her floppy t-shirt thinking about the task ahead of her.

She sat up in her bed and lifted her jeans off the bedroom floor. She put them on, and went to the bathroom in the hall to splash some water on her face. Looking at her reflection in the mirror, she could see her mother's green eyes and high cheekbones in her own face. They also shared the same blonde hair. Maybe, Samantha realized, she would stand as a living memorial to her mother, even if the house couldn't. She dried her face on a towel and headed downstairs for a bite of breakfast.

Samantha decided an English muffin with butter and strawberry jam would hit the spot. Her mother always kept homemade strawberry jam on hand. That's another thing Samantha would miss if they sold the house; her mother had quite an impressive garden of strawberries, blackberries and blueberries growing on her acre lot. Samantha loved helping her put up preserves in the summer. It was Marjorie who instilled her love for cooking. She wondered whether she would have gone to culinary school if she hadn't spent so much time in the kitchen growing up.

She put the English muffins in the toaster and went to the front door to retrieve the morning paper. She unfolded it and read the front page as she carried it back to the kitchen. The toaster popped, and Sam tossed the newspaper on the round oak kitchen table and went to retrieve the muffin. After preparing it the way she liked it, she settled down at the table to read.

The Savannah paper had a different feel to it than the *Atlanta Constitution,* a more laid back, tourist flavor. Without consciously doing it, Samantha found herself reading the employment section. She had a prestigious position as head chef in a prominent Atlanta restaurant. She hadn't even considered changing jobs, but when she saw the opening for a chef at the Ballastone Inn in the historic district, she stopped, reached for a pen on the table, and circled the advertisement. The fact that it probably wouldn't pay what she was accustomed to didn't even enter her mind. All she thought was how enjoyable it would be to work in such a quaint location. The workload would be lighter than the continuous streams of people who entered her restaurant back in Atlanta.

As she took a sip of orange juice, she contemplated working up a resume on her mother's computer and applying. She wouldn't need to earn as much if she lived here at her mother's house. Her idea from the night before returned, and it suddenly didn't seem so far fetched after all. Her lease on her apartment in Atlanta was up for renewal in another month anyway. If she got the position, or any position in Savannah, she could buy her brother's part of the house and stay here.

She decided to forgo rummaging through her mother's things for now. There would be plenty of time for that later. Instead, she carried the paper to her mother's study and started the computer. While it booted, she thought through her strategy. Surely someone with her impressive credentials could get this type of position. The primary danger was they would perceive her as overqualified. She decided to remedy that in her cover letter. She'd emphasize her desire to move back to

Savannah and lead a more relaxed lifestyle. Tie that with her abundant experience, and they would see her as an ideal candidate.

Samantha pulled up the website for the Ballastone to get a feel for what the inn was like and grew even more excited about the prospect. She worked for some time on her resume and cover letter, printed them and then hopped into the shower. She decided to hand deliver them so that she could get a look around the place. Viewing pictures helped some, but she wanted to step inside and perhaps have a chance to shake the hand of a decision maker.

Chapter 4

~ ✧ ~

Samantha listened to the radio as she drove her blue Celica through Savannah's downtown historic district. The cobblestone streets, blocked off into squares, comprised a design initially created in the 1700's by General James Edward Oglethorpe, the founder of Savannah. The grand mansions, impressive statues in the center of the squares and the Spanish moss hanging from the gnarly live oaks gave Savannah a unique feel. There was no other city like it. Samantha loved it. She'd loved it since childhood when her mother took her there for historic tours.

She still remembered the hot summer night fifteen years earlier when her Mom took her and Travis for a ride in one of the hearse ghost tours. They rode around the city, sitting there with their heads popping out of the top of the hearse, looking at the glowing city lights, the historic mansions and monuments. They listened to their guide spin ghostly yarns of a young man bricked into the wall of the Foley house, and men and women hanged from the gnarly live oaks.

Thinking back on that hearse tour long ago, it had been creepy then, but no one could pay her to ride around in a hearse now! Still, the city in spite of its ghostly past, held an unequaled charm that drew Samantha to it. It was the perfect combination of history, romance, and elegant mystery—especially at night.

She found an open spot along the street near the Ballastone and parallel parked. She approached the vine-covered building, put her hand on the cold wrought iron railing and started up the stone steps. The steps of the half-spiral staircase were close together, and Samantha noted that as worn smooth as they were they would be slick on a rainy day.

She reached for the ornate doorknob, turned and pushed. Inside she saw a 19th century parlor to the right and a small sitting area to the left. Straight ahead of her, two guests stood in front of the concierge's desk where an attractive black woman handed the man a key.

"Because we have limited parking, please place your car keys in the lock box associated with your room. That way if we need to move your car for someone to get out, we can do so without disturbing you," the woman said in a surprisingly accent-less voice as she pointed to a series of little wooden drawers behind her right shoulder.

The man handed her his keys, and she rose to her feet and placed them in one of the little drawers. "I'll show you to your room now," she said as she walked around them and started up a flight of stairs to Samantha's left.

"I'll be with you in a moment," the woman made eye contact with Samantha.

"No hurry," Samantha replied and then turned to examine a library table to her left where a plethora of brochures for local restaurants and tourist attractions lay.

Once the couple started up the stairs, Samantha took the

opportunity to snoop around a bit. She stepped back toward the parlor where a couch, coffee table and several wingback chairs were arranged on an oriental rug. A large fireplace stood along the far wall and little round breakfast tables perched by the windows along the outer walls. Samantha turned left and found an adjoining room with several small breakfast tables along the walls and a bar where a pitcher of lemonade and a plate of cookies had been set out for guests.

Just past the bar was a doorway that led back to the concierge's desk. She went through it and turned right. She noted an empty guest quarters. The door stood open revealing a king size canopy bed and a lavishly decorated room with wooden floors covered by a Parisian rug.

When she heard footsteps coming down the stairs, she came back to the desk and stood on the proper side of it to wait.

"Good morning," the concierge greeted, her genuinely happy grin revealing a set of straight white teeth.

"Good morning," Samantha smiled back.

"Are you checking in?" the woman inquired as she stepped around Samantha to the desk.

"Actually, I'm here to apply for the chef position that you had in the paper."

"Oh?"

"Yes, I just wanted to take a look around a little. It's a beautiful inn."

"Thank you."

"I'm Samantha Reynolds," Samantha extended her hand to the woman who stood behind the desk.

"Simone Childers," the young woman replied, taking Samantha's hand in a firm handshake.

"I'm actually thinking of moving back to Savannah from Atlanta where I've been a chef at The Chart House for the last four years. My mother just passed away, and I suppose it's given me a longing for home."

"My condolences on your loss," the woman offered sincerely, her brown eyes narrowing sympathetically.

Samantha gave her a weak smile, "Anyway, I won't keep you." She extended the sealed white envelope containing her resume. "Would you mind giving this to the appropriate individual?"

The woman took the envelope. "Wait one moment, and I'll see if Mr. Salandi has time to speak with you." Simone headed toward an office behind her.

"Well, if it's no trouble," Samantha quickly looked down at her navy jacket, straightened it a little and removed a fleck of lint from her shoulder.

Simone disappeared into the office and several minutes later she emerged with a tall, brown-haired man following behind her.

"Miss Reynolds," the man who appeared to be in his late forties extended his hand. "Your resume is quite impressive."

"Thank you, sir," Samantha replied, a bit surprised that he would have already looked at it.

"Would you care to have a look around the kitchen?" he offered.

"I'd love that," Samantha followed him back the way he'd

come and off to a back area of the inn which opened up into a spacious kitchen. It wasn't as large as the one she was accustomed to, but it didn't need to be. Samantha stepped inside and noted that it had all the best appliances and cookware.

"Miss Reynolds, this is Martha. Martha will be retiring in a few weeks." Martha's kind blue eyes met Samantha's. She adjusted the white bandana on her gray hair and stepped forward, extending her slender fingers.

"Martha," Samantha repeated and shook the woman's hand. "Nice to meet you."

After a tour of the kitchen, Mr. Salandi led Samantha back to his office. "Please have a seat," he motioned for her to sit in a chair. He took his place behind the desk across from her and began talking with her about her experience and plans for the future.

By the time Samantha emerged from the inn forty-five minutes later, she had the position at a healthy salary. With the money she'd saved, she could buy her brother's share of their mother's home.

Now she just needed to call Travis to see if he would sell. She knew he would, but they needed to work out the details. She went to her car, slid behind the wheel and punched Travis' number on her cell phone.

~ ✧ ~

"Sam, are you sure you want to do this? It seems a bit hasty," Travis raked his slender fingers through his thick blonde hair. He stood over his desk tapping his pencil eraser on an open scroll of architectural plans. "No, I'm not saying that at all. Of course Leslie and I would love to have you close by. I just think you need to think this through before you go giving up a good job in Atlanta."

Leslie entered his office door carrying their one-year-old on her hip.

"What's going on?" she whispered.

Travis lifted his hand, motioning for her to wait for an explanation. "Sam, are you still there? You're breaking up. Can you hear me?"

He released a sarcastic, "Great!" and placed the portable phone back on its cradle.

"What's wrong? You look upset," Leslie's blue eyes held concern.

"Oh, just typical Sam—making hasty decisions with her life." He shook his head.

"What do you mean?"

"She's quitting her job at the Chart House for a breakfast chef position at the Ballastone in the historic district."

"Really?" Leslie's eyes brightened excitedly. "So she's moving back here to Savannah?"

"Looks like it," Travis flopped down in his swivel chair and flung his pencil on the desk.

"Why aren't you happy? Sam's the only family you have—besides us, of course." She adjusted the baby boy on her hip. "Surely having her nearby is a good thing."

"It's not that. I just think she's making a bad career move. Not to mention she's got it in her head to buy my half of Mom's house and live there."

"Really? That's a great idea!" Leslie said excitedly.

"No, Leslie. It's not a great idea," Travis stared at his wife as if she were dim-witted.

"Why?"

"It's not healthy for Sam to live in that house—with all those memories. She'll never let go of Mom and move on with her life if she stays there."

"I don't think it's that bad." Leslie argued. "She'll be close, and we can get her out more, get her building a social life. You said she hasn't gotten out any since Jerry jilted her."

Travis cocked his head to one side, considering what his wife had said. "But don't you think it's sort of creepy the way she wants to preserve Mom's house like some kind of shrine to her?"

"It's just the initial shock. She'll let go of that idea in time. She's still grieving." She met his eyes seriously and added, "Both of you are. You need each other."

"Maybe," Travis mumbled. "I'm just afraid she's making another hasty decision that could really mess up her life."

"You mean like Jerry," Leslie said.

"Yeah, how long did she know that jerk before she decided to marry him? A month? She can't keep making decisions like that. She's got to start thinking things through." Travis patted his hand on his desk emphasizing the last three words.

"For the baby of the family, you sure are the practical one," Leslie winked at her husband and shifted the child to her other hip.

"Someone's got to be practical. Heaven knows it's never been Sam's strong point, and with Mom gone, I guess it's up to me to keep her head on straight." Travis propped his elbow on the desk and rested his head on his fist.

Leslie put a hand on her husband's shoulder, "Everything's going to be all right. I have a good feeling about this. Plus, with Sean Cooper free it might be the perfect time to get him and Samantha together."

Travis lifted his eyes to his wife doubtfully, "Sean and Sam are just friends."

"I don't think so," Leslie raised a single eyebrow as her lips curled into a grin.

"Don't start that matchmaking nonsense of yours, now. I grew up with Sean and Sam. I was there. They're just friends."

"That may be true, but it doesn't mean it stayed that way," her voice held a tone of insinuation indicating she held information Travis did not.

"What are you talking about?" Travis scrunched his nose, doubtful that his wife could know anything he did not about his sister and the city alderman, Sean Cooper.

"Oh, nothing," she shrugged nonchalantly and turned back to the door. "I've got a dirty diaper to change."

"Have fun," he quipped sarcastically as she left him alone with his thoughts.

Chapter 5

~ ✧ ~

Two weeks later . . .

Travis finished helping Samantha put the mattress on her bed frame. She'd moved her furniture into their mother's home and replaced some of Marjorie's older pieces with her own.

"I still think you should use Mom's room. It's bigger, plus it has the private bath," Travis suggested for at least the fourth time.

"I wouldn't feel right putting my furniture in her room," Samantha gave her usual reply.

"Then use it as it is," he countered.

Samantha shook her head negatively, "I couldn't sleep in that bed."

Travis grimaced, "Yeah, guess I wouldn't want to sleep in it either." He paused for a moment and took a deep breath, "Sam, are you absolutely certain you want to live here? Don't you think it's a little . . . creepy?"

"No, it feels like home. I feel close to Mom here." She looked around her old teenage room, satisfied with her remodeling of it. They'd carried the old furniture out to the garage so it looked like an adult's room now.

Travis sighed, "All right." He turned and walked to the

bedroom door. "Well, I told Leslie I'd be home for dinner by six-thirty."

"Yeah, you better get going," Samantha followed her brother into the hall and down the staircase. "Thanks for helping me with the move," Samantha hugged her brother as he stood by the front door preparing to leave.

"You're welcome," he patted her back. "And if this house gets to be too much for you, just say the word and you can come stay with Leslie and me until you can find another place.

"Thanks for the offer, but I know this is the right move for me," she looked up into her brother's concerned eyes. "Don't worry about me, Travis. I'll be just fine."

Travis nodded. "All right." He opened the door and stepped out. "We'll see you Sunday," he called over his shoulder as he made his way to his car.

"Looking forward to it." She waved, watched him get into his car and then shut the front door.

She looked to her left at the stacks of boxes in the living room. Travis had helped her carry some of her mother's older furniture out of the living room and put it in the garage. They replaced it with Samantha's new sofa, recliner, loveseat and big screen television.

Samantha's stomach growled. She went to the kitchen, letting her hand trace along her mother's oak table as she passed it. She didn't redecorate the kitchen. There were too many fond memories she didn't want to disturb.

Samantha set to work making her dinner; pecan crusted salmon on a bed of orzo with a spinach and mandarin orange salad on the side. As she sat down at the kitchen table in front of her meal and looked across to the empty chair, moisture filled her eyes. She closed them, leaning her head in her hands. She could almost feel her mother's arm around her shoulders. It felt so real that she closed her eyes and whispered, "Mom" into the silence.

The sensation lingered a few seconds longer, then it was gone. She opened her eyes, but found no one. If her stomach hadn't grumbled, reminding her that she hadn't eaten anything since breakfast, she would have pushed the plate aside. Instead she stood up, lifted her plate and cup and carried them to the living room. She set them on the coffee table and turned on the television. She'd find the strength to eat at that table another night, but not tonight.

Samantha let the evening pass watching a funny movie and then headed for bed. She paused at her mother's open door. Hadn't she closed it earlier in the afternoon? She shook her head. She and Travis were moving so many things in and out that maybe one of them left it open. She reached for the knob and closed the door.

~ ✧ ~

The next morning, Samantha rose early for her first day working at the Ballastone. She showered, dressed and was out the door by four-thirty. Even though breakfast wasn't served until eight, she wanted to make sure she got there in plenty of time and learned her way around the kitchen.

She parked in the employee area and made her way to the

back door of the building. She lifted the phone and announced herself to the concierge.

"Hi Samantha, glad to have you aboard," Simone gave her a cheery greeting and the door unlocked.

Samantha stepped inside, went up the flight of stairs and toward the kitchen.

She flipped on the light and started familiarizing herself with the facilities. She looked at the note Mr. Salandi left on the counter. She was to serve a choice of egg's Benedict, French toast, and fruit cups along with freshly squeezed orange juice, coffee and danishes. She had her work cut out for her, but she was used to working quickly.

She started pulling ingredients from the refrigerator and pantry and set to work. A few minutes into her task, Simone appeared at the doorway. "How's everything going?"

"Good," Samantha smiled as she mixed her pastry dough.

"Here are your keys to the building. This one is for the back door and this one is for the kitchen. I opened up for you this morning, but this will let you get in and out whenever you need to." Simone set the keys on the food preparation counter.

"Thanks."

"I just need you to sign right here that you received them," Simone set a clipboard on the counter.

Samantha dusted her hands together to remove the excess flour and then removed her latex gloves and signed the form.

"Thanks," Simone smiled. "Have fun and let me know if you need anything."

"I will," Samantha nodded, and Simone left the kitchen.

The breakfast preparations went well and the morning passed swiftly. Soon Samantha was serving guests along with Kay, her assistant who arrived at seven.

Guests at the Ballastone had the choice of eating indoors or out. They could eat at one of the many circular tables placed beside the windows of the main floor, or they could step outside and enjoy their meal at the tables in the garden area. Savannah, being on the southern Atlantic coast of Georgia, provided beautiful weather year-round for outdoor eating. But this morning it was drizzling, so everyone remained indoors.

After all the guests were served, Mr. Salandi stepped into the kitchen, wearing a smile on his face. His brown eyes twinkled. "Everyone's raving about your Danishes. I decided to see if you had any left over for me to try."

"Of course, sir." Samantha used a set of tongs to place a blueberry pastry on a plate for him. "I didn't realize you were here or I could have made you a plate."

"No, I just got here." He took the plate and ate a bite of pastry. "Oh," he nodded. "This is delicious."

"Aren't they wonderful?" Kay said as she entered the kitchen carrying a tray of empty dishes.

"Definitely," Mr. Salandi agreed. "Can't wait to see what you come up with for high tea."

"Thank you," Samantha smiled, glad to be appreciated. She knew it was just the novelty of being the new chef. Once they got used to her, they wouldn't be so surprised and the compliments would subside. At least that's what had happened with her boss at the Chart House. The customers still left their compliments, but her boss had grown to expect constant perfection from her. Issuing compliments wasn't part of his management style, especially in the last couple years.

"Mr. Nielson is here to see you, sir," Simone poked her head into the kitchen.

"Tell him I'll be right there." Mr. Salandi wiped his mouth with a napkin. "Could you please prepare a plate for Mr. Nielson?"

"I'll take care of that," Kay offered and set to work.

Samantha thanked her and then went to the pantry to retrieve the ingredients for the cookies she planned to make for afternoon tea. Mr. Salandi left the kitchen and went back to greet his guest. Kay followed shortly after and found Mr. Salandi and Mr. Nielson sitting at one of the tables in the bar.

"Here's your breakfast, Mr. Nielson. I hope you enjoy it," she said as she placed the plate and a glass of juice in front of him. She served the two men coffee and then left them to their conversation.

"How have you been, Geoffrey?" Mr. Salandi asked.

"It's been a little rough the last few weeks," the man nodded somberly.

Jim Salandi's face showed genuine concern, "Is everything all right?"

"A friend of mine passed away suddenly a couple weeks ago, and it's just been difficult," Geoffrey Nielson opened his napkin and laid it across the trousers of his gray Armani suit.

"I'm so sorry to hear that. Anyone I know?" Jim Salandi's eyes narrowed with concern.

"No, I don't believe so," Geoffrey shook his head, but it did not disturb his shortly cropped black hair that grayed at the temples. "It was a woman I was seeing. It all happened rather suddenly."

"Car accident?" Mr. Salandi prompted.

"No, heart attack. She was just too young for something like that," Geoffrey rubbed his brow.

"I'm so sorry," Salandi offered.

"Yes, well, what can be done?" Geoffrey shrugged and took a bite of his Danish. His eyebrows rose with pleasure, "This is excellent! Did Martha make this?"

"Martha retired," Mr. Salandi replied. "This is my new chef."

"Well, I must meet this chef of yours," Geoffrey said.

Jim Salandi smiled, eager to please Savannah's City Manager. Geoffrey Nielson threw some of the most lavish events in the city, and Jim had been trying to book one of his parties for years. "She is excellent. She was the head chef at the Chart House in Atlanta."

"How did you manage that?" Geoffrey inquired as Jim waved at Kay. Kay came immediately toward her employer.

"Could you please ask Samantha to come out for a moment? I'd like her to meet Mr. Nielson," Jim asked her.

"Yes sir," Kay nodded and left.

"She was tired of Atlanta and wanted to come back to Savannah," Jim answered Geoffrey's previous question.

"Well aren't you the lucky one," Geoffrey took a sip of his coffee. He choked a little on it when Samantha stepped through the doorway. He cleared his throat and patted his napkin to his lips.

Jim stood and pulled another chair to their table, "Samantha, I'd like you to meet Mr. Geoffrey Nielson, our City Manager here in Savannah. Geoffrey, this is Miss Samantha Reynolds."

Jim didn't miss the strange expression of acknowledgment in Geoffrey's eyes as he took Samantha's hand, "Miss Reynolds." As Samantha took her seat Geoffrey asked, "So is everything you cook this delicious?"

Samantha offered a humble smile.

"Yes, it is," Jim answered for her.

Geoffrey turned his attention to the innkeeper, "Jim, I'm having a little last minute get-together for the members of the city council this Friday afternoon. I know it's short notice, but I'd like the Ballastone to cater it. Would that work for you?"

"Certainly," Jim agreed.

When the two men looked at Samantha, she smiled and said, "I would be honored."

"Good, now, what are your suggestions? I want to keep it light. It'll be around two o'clock," Geoffrey began and the three of them spent the next thirty minutes discussing the menu for the event.

By the time Samantha returned to the kitchen, she was running behind schedule, but it was worth it. This was quite an opportunity for her to serve the city council of Savannah. She smiled to herself as she put a batch of cookies in the oven. Not only was she looking forward to seeing her old friend Sean Cooper who would be at the event, but also she couldn't wait to inform Travis that her position at the Ballastone wasn't such a step down after all.

Chapter 6

~ ✧ ~

Lance Nielson raked his calloused hand through his sandy blonde hair as he knocked on the front door of the stately Savannah mansion. His parents had purchased the restored piece of 18th century architecture in the 1990's before his father became City Manager. It didn't feel like home to Lance, who had grown up in a typical three-bedroom rancher in the suburbs. His father's sudden business success in the late 80's had brought about a lot of changes for his family, none of which Lance deemed good.

When the butler opened the door, the somber gentleman looked down at Lance's work boots and jeans and then up to his blue Oxford that hung loosely open over a white tank top.

"Your father's rather busy with guests at the moment," came the butler's stiff reply.

"I saw the cars," Lance answered. "I'll just hang out in the kitchen until he's free." He stepped inside, not waiting for the butler to move back.

The servant opened the door a little wider, allowing Lance more room to pass. Not waiting for guidance, Lance headed straight back through the house to the kitchen in the rear.

Lance put his hand to his stomach when it growled. He

hadn't had lunch yet, and he knew he could always count on some delicious food when his father threw one of his parties. He hadn't come intentionally for the food, but it definitely was a bonus.

He tromped through the hallway and pushed open the swinging kitchen door. Just as he did so, Samantha was on her way through with a tray of stuffed mushrooms. She stepped back, braced the tray and barely kept it from spilling onto the floor.

"I'm sorry," Lance put his hand on her elbow to steady her. When his brown eyes met hers, they narrowed a little. "Do . . . Do I know you?" he stammered after she'd regained her balance.

"I don't believe so," she replied.

At that moment, Kay walked down the hallway and stopped next to Lance. "I'll take that, Samantha," she offered and Samantha handed it to her.

Kay turned and left and Lance extended his hand, "I'm Lance Nielson. Geoffrey Nielson is my father."

"Nice to meet you. I'm Samantha Reynolds, from the Ballastone," she smiled and shook his hand.

"Reynolds?" his eyes widened with enlightenment. "Are you Marjorie Reynolds' daughter?"

Samantha's face paled slightly, "Yes, yes I am."

"I was so sorry to hear about your mother. She was a wonderful lady. The only woman my dad ever dated that I liked." He placed a second hand over hers as he held her grip a moment longer.

"Dated? My mom was seeing your dad?" Lance watched the blonde's face grow perplexed.

"You didn't know that?" His eyes narrowed, surprised that she wasn't aware of the fact.

"No," Samantha's expression grew more puzzled. "When did they date? It must not have been for long," She slipped her hand from his.

"For about the last three months before she passed away. Dad was pretty shook up there for a couple weeks."

"Hmmm . . . I had no idea." She seemed to be searching her memory for any recollection of her mother having dated the City Manager. "Was he at the funeral?"

"We were both there, but then there was quite a crowd." Lance shrugged.

"Hmm," Samantha nodded, still obviously perplexed.

"Kind of odd she wouldn't mention it. They went everywhere together," he stepped past her and headed toward the kitchen sink. "Then again, your mother never was a name dropper." He rolled up his shirt sleeves and turned on the water.

"Well, I just moved back to Savannah from Atlanta a couple weeks ago, so maybe that's why," Samantha turned and watched him wash his hands.

"Care if I grab a bite?" Lance gestured toward the food preparation island laden with appetizers.

"Help yourself," she went back to her work at the island and began filling another tray.

Lance took a mushroom and popped it in his mouth. He watched her as he chewed the delicious morsel. She certainly did look a lot like Marjorie! They could pass for sisters.

Samantha's head shook a little, clearly thrown by the information he'd just given her. "I still can't believe she didn't tell me this."

"Well," Lance shrugged. "Maybe she didn't think it was worth talking about."

"Seeing the City Manager for three months?" Samantha's voice lilted with incredulity.

"Maybe she wasn't as impressed with him as he was with her," Lance stated dryly. He turned toward the cabinet, removed a glass and filled it at the kitchen sink. He stared out the back window at his father who was carrying on a serious conversation with an alderman on the patio. "I've never been all that impressed with him," he muttered.

"Pardon me?" Samantha asked.

"Nothing," he glanced over his shoulder at her then took a sip of his water. He carried it back to where she worked. "You know, you really look an awful lot like your mother. It's uncanny."

"Thank you. I take that as a compliment." Samantha smiled and Lance felt a wave of attraction. Her smile only served to magnify her beauty.

"You should. Your mother was beautiful." He grabbed a finger sandwich and bit into it.

"So what do you do? You don't seem too interested in hobnobbing with politicians," Samantha observed.

"That obvious—eh?" His brown eyes twinkled as they met hers. "Nope, don't care a thing about hobnobbing with politicians. But I do enjoy the food they eat." He reached for a puffed pastry. "I'm a foreman for a local construction company."

"Ah, so that's why you have such a hearty appetite," she teased.

Lance smiled, "You have your mom's dry wit too." He could tell he'd touched her with that compliment. Her green eyes held a spark of pleasant melancholy. "But now this pastry" he held it up and pointed at it. "This is all your own. I've never tasted anything this fabulous in my life."

She chuckled lightly, "Thank you . . . Well, I guess I better get serving," she smiled and carried the tray out of the kitchen.

Lance watched her tall, slender form leave the kitchen. The woman was talented, but was that why his father hired her? And why hadn't he said anything to her about knowing Marjorie? Then again, Lance reminded himself, he never understood how his father's mind worked. Why should he start now?

~ ✧ ~

Samantha carried the tray out to the back patio where several men in suits stood talking with one another. Their wives sat around patio tables conversing and sipping drinks. Samantha tried to picture her mother at such a party. She would have fit in easily enough, but it wasn't the kind of thing she imagined her mother enjoying. While the men took the hors-d'oeuvres from the tray, Samantha's eyes scanned the room looking for someone in particular.

As her gaze shifted around the room, her eyes met Sean's and he started in her direction. She noticed how his business suit hung handsomely on his broad shoulders and trim waist.

Too bad he'd decided on bachelorhood.

"Samantha!" Sean put his hand on her arm and leaned in to kiss her cheek. "You look fantastic."

"Thanks," she could feel herself blushing, and she suddenly wished she wasn't holding a serving tray and that Sean wasn't making such a big deal over her. A few people were already looking in their direction.

"So you're the mastermind behind this delicious food?" he asked.

She nodded. Samantha suddenly remembered her mother's last words to her—that she should contact Sean if anything happened. Samantha couldn't get into a conversation with him about that here. Besides, couldn't the other people in the law office deal with paperwork? Her mother was always meticulous and a bit of a control freak. It would have been just like her to have a premonition of her own death and then worry about whether someone filed paperwork properly after she was gone!

"I didn't know you were at the Ballastone? Are you here to stay?" Sean's hand lingered on Samantha's forearm in a caressing motion.

She nodded again. His nearness had made her go tongue-tied.

"Hey, no monopolizing the chef," Geoffrey interjected as he came to stand beside Sean and Sam. He reached for a puffed pastry from her tray.

"I'm sorry, sir. I do need to get back to work," she apologized.

"No, that's all right," Geoffrey put his hand to her back. "So, you two know each other?" He looked from Sean Cooper to Samantha and back.

"We went to high school together," Sean answered. "I guess you know that her mother was Marjorie Reynolds"

Geoffrey nodded somberly, "It's been hard without her."

Samantha stared at the sad expression in his eyes. "I know it seems odd, sir, but until your son mentioned it, I didn't even know you two were seeing each other."

"You know my son?" Geoffrey's eyebrows lowered with puzzlement.

"I met him in the kitchen."

"Oh," he nodded. "Well, Marjorie and I had only been seeing each other a short while. I would have introduced myself at the funeral, but there were so many people, and you and your brother were clearly grieving. I just . . ."

"I understand," she offered him the smile she'd given to at least a hundred people in the last two weeks when they lost words trying to express their condolences.

"Sean," she put her hand on his arm. "It was great seeing you again." She started to dismiss herself and get back to work.

"You'll have to give me your number," Sean interjected before she could leave.

"I'm staying at Mom's house. So it's the same number it's always been. 554—"

"2745," Sean and Geoffrey finished for her in unison. The two men looked at each other and laughed.

"Give me a call anytime," she smiled and carried her tray over to a table where four women were gossiping and sipping martinis.

Samantha served guests until her tray was empty. When she went back to the kitchen to refill it, Lance had left. She had expected to find him there, having eaten a tray of appetizers. She smiled to herself thinking about his boyish, yet ruggedly handsome way of helping himself to the food. He seemed quite different from his father, and she deduced that he must take after his mother.

Thinking of Lance's mother, she wondered what had happened to her. Evidently Geoffrey Nielson was single. Otherwise he wouldn't be so openly dating her mother. Not to mention, she knew her mother didn't date married men.

Their relationship had clearly been a public one. While serving, at least three people stopped Samantha and commented on her resemblance to Marjorie and offered their condolences.

Samantha still thought it odd that her mother had never mentioned Geoffrey. Frankly, Samantha felt a little hurt that she hadn't confided in her. Why hadn't she said anything over Christmas? Then again, they had been busy and her mother spent most of her time trying to match-make Samantha and Sean. Samantha decided she'd give Travis a call when she got home and find out just how much he knew about this relationship.

Samantha and Kay finished serving all the guests, cleaned up the kitchen and rode back together to the Ballastone in the catering van. It was after six by the time she got home. She'd been on her feet all day and decided to soak in a tub for a while before calling Travis. He'd have more time to talk after dinner anyway.

The whirlpool was in the master bath. As uneasy as she felt about going into her mother's room, she needed the relaxation of the whirlpool. So she opened the door and headed straight for the bathroom, not giving herself time to get maudlin. She started the water and then went back to her room to gather a change of clothes and the portable phone. She carried them back into the bathroom, slipped out of her clothes and into the tub.

The jets felt great on her tired, aching muscles. She'd been on her feet more today than usual. She'd worked at the Ballastone and then gone straight to Nielson's. As she lay there, relaxing, her mind wandered to Sean. He'd looked so handsome this afternoon. Too bad he wanted to focus on his career and had sworn off women.

Her mind went back to that last night they were together before she left for culinary school. She remembered sitting on her front porch talking, listening to the crickets, and gazing at the stars while they discussed their plans for the future. The memory brought with it the sweet scent of magnolia blossoms hanging thick in the humid summer night. When Sean stood to leave, he walked her to her door, and that's when Samantha discovered that there was something much deeper between the two of them than friendship.

He hugged her, then leaned in to give her a quick kiss goodbye. What started out as a friendly gesture quickly turned into a romantic interlude that lasted much longer. She'd kissed other young men in high school, but there was nothing to compare with the deep emotional bond she felt with Sean. And she knew he sensed it too.

She could still hear his husky whisper, "Why haven't we ever done this before?"

Dazed and a bit unnerved by the emotions tingling through her body, all she could do was shrug and stare up into his blue eyes.

Sean leaned over and kissed her lightly, hugged her and whispered, "Write me" into her ear. Then he was gone.

Over the years, her mother kept her abreast of what was happening in Sean's life, but every time Samantha came home interested in seeing him, he was involved with someone else. The times he'd call her wanting to get together, she was seeing another man. The timing had always been off. But now . . . maybe now that they were both free . . . then again, Sean seemed determined to avoid a relationship.

The phone rang. Immediately Samantha hoped it would be Sean. He'd still remembered her number after all these years. Maybe it was him. It rang again. She turned off the jets, dried her hands on a towel and picked up the phone.

"Hello," she could hear the hopefulness in her own voice.

"Sam."

"Oh, Hi, Travis."

"Don't sound so disappointed," he teased with mock hurt in his voice.

"I'm not disappointed. What's up?"

"Just called to see how things went this afternoon," he said.

Samantha let her hand ride along the surface of the water.

"It went great. Everyone seemed to like the food."

"That's wonderful, Sam!"

"So did you know that Mom had been dating Geoffrey Nielson?" she asked the question that had been on her mind for hours.

"Yeah, didn't you?"

"No." Samantha shook her head even though Travis couldn't see her do it.

"Huh," Travis muttered. "Well, it wasn't any big deal. They had just been seeing each other for a few months"

"Nielson's son acted like his father was really torn up over what happened to Mom."

"Well, anyone would be in his position, but I don't think their relationship was all that serious." Travis explained.

"What was their relationship? And why do you think she never mentioned it to me?"

"I think it was pretty shallow to be honest with you, and that's probably the reason she didn't say anything about it."

"What do you mean by shallow?" Sam moved the phone to her other ear.

"I mean, they both knew they looked good with each other. Nielson was good for Mom's career. And Mom was just the kind of pretty woman Nielson wanted on his arm," Travis theorized.

"I can't see Mom dating someone just to further her career," Samantha retorted.

"Well, I hate to disagree with you, but in this case, I think you're wrong."

"Why?" Samantha hit the speaker button on the portable phone and laid it down on the vanity. She released the drain and stood up. The water gurgled out and the moisture on her body dripped noisily into the tub.

"Are you in the tub? I can call you back."

"No, I have you on speaker. Go ahead, why do you think she was dating Geoffrey to further her career?" Sam stepped out and dried herself with a pink towel.

"I don't know. I guess I don't have any hard facts to prove it. I just got the idea that there was something else going on there, something business-like." Travis paused before continuing. "She was stiffer around Nielson than I've seen her with anyone, yet she kept going out with him."

"Stiffer?" Samantha repeated for clarification.

"I can't put it into words. It was just forced. When I asked her about him, she said it probably wasn't going anywhere, but she was giving it time."

"That just doesn't sound like Mom," Samantha wrapped the towel around her head and started putting on her clothes. "I still can't believe she never mentioned him to me."

"Why don't you look around her room and find her journal? She wrote everything in that thing." Travis suggested.

Samantha pondered that idea for a moment, "I don't know. Seems like an invasion of privacy."

"You didn't care about invading her privacy when you were sixteen and reading it," Travis teased.

"That was different. I'm a grown woman now." Sam rubbed her hair with the towel.

"Yeah, a grown woman who's better able to handle what she finds in her mother's journal."

"I don't know, Travis. It just doesn't seem right."

"Look, Sam," Travis reasoned. "She's gone. She's off singing with choirs of angels. She's not going to care whether you read her journal or not. Mom would rather you read it than sit there and drive yourself nuts wondering why she didn't confide in you."

"That's just it, she didn't confide in me. And I don't understand why." An aching sensation needled Samantha's heart. She realized it was probably her own fault. She'd been so self-absorbed with her own situation with Sean over the Christmas holiday that she hadn't taken the time to ask her mother about her life. Then again, why hadn't her mother mentioned Nielson in one of their regular weekly phone calls?

"Look for the journal, Sam," Travis interrupted her thoughts.

"But if she didn't confide in me, she evidently didn't want me to know." Sam rubbed a towel along the floor with her foot, wiping up the excess water.

"Sam, she would have told you eventually. Just find it. Read it." Travis sounded like he was giving her an order rather than a suggestion.

"All right," Samantha acquiesced. "I'll look around."

Chapter 7

~ ✧ ~

Samantha knew just where Marjorie kept her journal, at least where she used to keep it—between her mattress and box spring. She went to the bed, shoved her hand under the mattress and felt around. Finding nothing, she went to the opposite side of the queen size bed and felt beneath the mattress. There it was—a brown leather journal.

Marjorie never knew that Samantha, at age sixteen, snuck and read her journal. It was a good thing too, because if Marjorie had known, she would have selected a new hiding place.

She plopped down on her mother's bed and opened the book. The thought occurred to her that perhaps she should leave the room, but it seemed like the appropriate place to read the journal. It reminded her of the evenings she'd lie on this same bed and have long talks about a basketball game or her latest crush. It seemed only fitting that her mother's secrets be shared in the same place.

She thumbed through the journal until she came to October, at about the time she should have started dating Geoffrey. She found the entry. She'd met him at the office. He was there to sign a contract with a client. After everyone left, he asked her out for dinner and she agreed. She didn't go into any details about her first impression of him, just mentioned that he planned to take her to dinner and the opera and how she was looking forward to seeing *Tristan and Isolde*.

Samantha went on to the next entry. It was about herself. Her mother recorded portions of a conversation she'd had with Samantha encouraging her to get out and date more, that she'd been pining away for Jerry for far too long. Marjorie expressed her concerns about her daughter, and Samantha could feel the tears brimming in her eyes, her mother's love for her evident in the journal entry.

Samantha continued on through the journal, but the entries were more like a travelogue than a record of Marjorie's feelings for Geoffrey. They went to dinner parties, out on his yacht, to concerts and the opera. She recorded what she enjoyed about a particular piece of music or about how beautiful the day was on the Atlantic, but nothing much about Geoffrey.

Around December 16th she wrote something that made Samantha stop and re-read it, "It's almost as if Geoffrey is two people at times. He can be kind and accommodating, then occasionally he becomes withdrawn and defensive like he did tonight. I'm beginning to think there's no future in this relationship."

Samantha kept reading, hoping there would be further explanation, but there wasn't. She gave no details about what had occurred that evening.

The next few days' entries were work related. Marjorie was snowed under with complex city government contracts. Several corporations her firm represented were involved with the contracts, and she felt like she barely had time to breathe. Sam skimmed over these entries that appeared to be primarily business-related and skipped to the last entry on December 28th, the very night she died.

"I'm exhausted," she wrote. "It's been a long day, piles of paperwork to catch up on from over the holidays. There's a concern at work over the government contracts, involves Geoffrey and Leland Norris. I've set up an appointment to talk with Sean Cooper about it tomorrow. Maybe he can help me figure it out. Sean was always a good young man. I know I can trust him. Oh well, I'm going to watch a movie and try to get my mind off it."

Samantha read and reread the paragraph over and over. What was her mother going to talk to Sean about? She wrote of trusting him. She'd said almost the same thing to Samantha the day she died. At the time Samantha thought her mother meant that she could trust Sean in a relationship and that he wouldn't abandon her like Jerry did. But maybe she meant something else.

She wanted to pick up the phone and call him, but she didn't know his home number. She reached for a phone book and tried to look him up, but only found his office. His home phone was unlisted.

Samantha called his office, but only got his voice mail. She listened to his attractive voice, paused, and debated on leaving a message. She decided against it—she'd just wait and call back tomorrow. After making herself some food, she settled into her bed for the evening, listened to music and read through her mother's journal.

~ ✧ ~

The next day during her lunch break, Samantha stopped by a local bakery to get a bagel for lunch. When she stepped inside, she was surprised to see Lance Nielson standing at the counter. He handed the cashier a few bills and the woman handed him his change. Samantha watched him slip his leather wallet into the back pocket of his jeans, and felt a twinge of attraction. He shifted his boot, putting all his weight on his right leg and leaned his elbow on the counter as he waited for the woman to make two turkey and Swiss bagels.

"Mr. Nielson," Samantha spoke from behind.

He turned to face her, "Miss Reynolds, good to see you again. How have been?"

"Good. You?"

"Great now that I've got something to eat," he took a brown paper sack from the woman and held it up.

Samantha smiled, remembering the boyish way Lance had raided the appetizers at his father's house the prior afternoon. Samantha stepped up to the counter, gave the woman her order and turned toward Lance.

"Didn't get enough yesterday then?" she smiled.

"Oh, I had plenty, but today's a new day." He lingered, waiting for her to receive her food.

"Care to join me for lunch?" he asked.

"Sure," she followed him to a booth by the window.

"Pretty day for working outside," Samantha commented as she looked out at the sunny afternoon and the cars going up and down the street.

"It is. I worked up quite an appetite," he pulled his bagels from the bag and unwrapped them.

"How long have you worked in construction?" Samantha asked.

"About ten years now—went straight into it after high school. I never was much of one for school."

"So you didn't go to college?" she asked.

"No, but it hasn't hurt me." Lance shrugged. "Business is going well."

"That's good."

"So tell me about yourself," he prompted then took a bite of his sandwich.

"There's not much to tell really," she shrugged.

"Oh come on, I know better than that. How'd you learn to cook the way you do?"

Sam smiled. "I went to culinary school in Atlanta. I also took a summer and studied in France. That was fun."

"Bet you learned a lot there." He took a bite of his bagel.

"I did."

He finished chewing and then wiped his mouth with a napkin. "Dad said you'd just moved back here from Atlanta."

"I've been in Atlanta since graduating from culinary school. I was working as a chef at the Chart House, but when Mom died, I decided to come back here."

"Do you have other family here?" he asked.

"My brother, Travis and his family. Actually, you might know him. He's an architect—Travis Reynolds," She answered.

Lance nodded. "I believe I've seen some of his work. He does a lot of restoration projects, doesn't he?"

"Yes," she nodded.

"He's good."

"He's meticulous, and very practical," Samantha expounded.

"I can see that in his work." They each took bites of their sandwiches. Then Lance pointed to her right hand. "So you're not married."

She shook her head, "No. You?"

"No."

"Ever been?" she asked.

"No, never found the right woman. You?"

"No," she dabbed her napkin to her lips.

"So since neither of us is married, how about we grab dinner and a movie tonight?" Lance suggested.

Samantha blushed a little at his directness, "Well, I . . . uh." She considered his offer for a moment. Her curiosity about her mother's relationship with Geoffrey was piqued, and Lance would probably be a good source of information.

"Do you have something better to do?" he asked.

"No, I guess not," she shrugged.

"Then how about I pick you up around six?" He wadded up his napkin and tossed it in his bag.

Samantha still felt hesitant. After all, she hadn't been out with anyone since Jerry. But the words of her mother's journal ran through her mind, and she decided it might be fun. Lance was cute and he came from a respectable family. Her mother knew him and hadn't written anything disparaging about him in her journal. Why not?

"Okay," she agreed.

"Great," he smiled. "So do you like crab? I know a really good place."

"I love it," she said.

Samantha and Lance sat there planning what movie they wanted to see, finished their lunch and each headed back to work. Samantha entered the Ballastone with a spring in her step. She liked Lance. Not only was he handsome, but also he had a fun personality. Normally, she would have felt nervous going out on her first date since being jilted, but Lance had such a laid-back quality about him, he set her at ease.

~ ✧ ~

"You look unusually chipper. Did you have a good lunch?" Kay asked when she came into the kitchen to find Samantha mixing cookies, singing along with the radio and dancing.

Samantha stopped instantly upon realizing she'd been discovered. "Oh," she chuckled. "Old habits die hard I guess. You caught me."

"Go right ahead, looks like you're having fun," Kay pulled her long auburn hair back into a ponytail and slipped a white scarf over her hair. "So what's put you in such a good mood?"

"I have a date." She smiled with a certain measure of pride, knowing her mother would be pleased if she were still alive.

"Really? Anyone I know?"

"Lance Nielson."

"The guy from the catering job yesterday?" Kay's mouth drew up into an amused expression. "The one who kept eating all the appetizers in the kitchen?"

"Yeah, I think he's kind of fun," Samantha replied playfully.

"And good looking," Kay added with a wink.

"That too," Samantha agreed as she placed a tray of cookies in the oven.

"So did he call you?" Kay asked.

"No, I bumped into him at the Bagel Bakery, and we ate lunch together," Sam summarized.

"When are you going out?" Kay asked as she began helping Sam roll cookies.

"Tonight."

"He doesn't let grass grow, does he? Two dates in the same day!" Kay exclaimed.

"The first wasn't a date," Samantha corrected.

"Still," Kay grabbed some cookie dough and shaped it into a ball. "I thought you were interested in the alderman?" Kay reminded Samantha of the conversation they'd had about Sean on the way home from Nielson's the day before.

"I am," Samantha replied, and Kay cocked a single eyebrow. "What?" Samantha retorted, then leaned her hands on the counter. "It's been a year since I've been out. I rushed into the last relationship. This time I think I'd like to sample from a few different plates, if you know what I mean."

Kay chuckled and nodded her head, "Fair enough. Sounds like a good idea. Sometimes I wish I'd sampled from a few more plates before I rushed into marriage at nineteen."

Samantha studied Kay's expression, "So you and your husband . . ."

"Oh, we get along great. Randy's a good husband and father.

I just got married so young, and I hadn't dated that much. I just wonder sometimes. You start pushing forty and you think maybe you shouldn't have gotten in such a big hurry."

"Don't even think that way," Samantha warned. "If you've got a good man, keep him and don't be looking back. Consider yourself lucky. There are some real losers out there."

"I know," Kay nodded. "You're right. Hopefully, you'll find a good one this time."

"I'm in no rush. Just sticking my toe in the water." Samantha rolled the cookie dough in her hands and started singing along with the radio again.

Chapter 8

~ ✧ ~

"So I told you about myself. What about you?" Samantha prompted as she sat across from Lance at a booth in the Crab Shack.

Lance shrugged, "What do you want to know?"

"I look at you and you're just so laid back and down-to-earth. How did you come out of a wealthy home like that, with the powerful father you have and be like you are?"

Lance responded with a wry grin, "My family wasn't always wealthy. In fact, we lived in the suburbs in a small three-bedroom rancher until my senior year. My dad was a partner in a construction company that did restorations on old Savannah real estate. My mom was a schoolteacher. Dad didn't come into money until about ten years ago when his business took off."

"Really? That's fascinating," Samantha watched him clasp his hands on the table. They were strong, callous hands of a man who'd worked hard to earn a living.

"So, I moved out right after graduation, went to work in my dad's construction company and have been on my own ever since. My parents bought the house Dad lives in shortly after I left, so I've really never been a part of that life."

"Are you close to your parents?"

"My dad and I have our good days and bad—probably more bad than good. I guess I just don't understand how he thinks," Lance shook his head with a gesture of frustration.

"What about your mom?"

"Mom and I were very close. A lot of people say I look and act like her," Lance answered with a melancholy expression.

Samantha couldn't help but notice that Lance used the phrase "were very close." She paused a moment, searching for the right words, "So your mom is . . ."

"She passed away a couple years ago. She had an ongoing heart problem that finally got the best of her."

"Oh, I'm so sorry, I know how hard it is to lose your mother," she reached her hand across the table and placed it over his. It was an instinctive reaction of comfort, which he accepted. He shifted his right hand, moving it warmly over hers. Their eyes met in unspoken communication, and Samantha knew that Lance understood what she was going through. Her eyes misted, and she felt simultaneously relieved and disappointed when the waitress interrupted the moment to set two heaping plates of crab legs in front of them.

They released each other's hands. "Thank you," Lance mumbled to the waitress.

Without speaking, both of them picked up a crab leg and cracked it open. As Lance snapped his, a piece of crab went sailing across the table and hit the window. Samantha watched the meat bounce off the glass and land on the table. Her twinkling eyes met his and they both broke into laughter.

The tension breaker made Sam a little bolder and she put her hand on the table. "Lance," she shook her head, still grinning. "I've had something on my mind since yesterday, and I just have to ask it."

"Sure, go ahead." He gestured for her to continue.

"I just can't picture my mom with someone like your dad. It's not that he's a bad guy; he just seems like he wouldn't be her type."

Lance showed neither offense nor surprise at the question. He chuckled lightly, "Personally, I couldn't see the attraction either. I mean, I can see why Dad wanted to be with Marjorie, just not the other way around. Your mom was too good for him."

"My brother thinks Mom dated Geoffrey to further her career." Samantha shook her head negatively. "But I just can't imagine Mom doing something like that."

Lance's expression grew pensive, "I really don't think that was it either. Your Mom wasn't like that. There had to be some attraction there, otherwise I don't think she would have been with him."

"Well, your dad is a very handsome man, and I'm sure she enjoyed the places they went together. But do you know if they got along?" Samantha was thinking of the journal entry that Marjorie made about Geoffrey being withdrawn and defensive at times.

"Your mom was a classy lady, Sam. She didn't pout or manipulate like a lot of women dad's dated. But they did have their arguments . . . well at least one that I know of."

"Really? What was it about?" She took a bite of crab.

"I was out at the house one afternoon swimming in the indoor pool. Sometimes I like to go over there and swim. My dad's always been fond of boats—even before he had money—so—I'm a fish," he chuckled. "Anyway, I got out of the pool, dried off and came upstairs. I was on my way out when I passed dad's office and heard him and Marjorie having . . . well . . . a bit of a heated discussion.

"Did you hear what it was about?" Samantha prompted.

"They'd been out to dinner that night, and when Dad went to pay, he pulled out his credit card and put it with the bill. Then he excused himself to go to the restroom. When he did, your mom was curious about just how much Dad had paid for the meal, so she opened the bill holder and noticed that the credit card Dad used wasn't his own."

"It wasn't?" Samantha interrupted. "Whose was it?"

"It belonged to Leland Norris," Lance answered.

"Leland Norris? The reclusive land developer?" Sam's voice lifted with surprise.

"Yeah," Lance nodded. "So your Mom was curious and asked Dad about it."

"A natural response," Samantha observed.

"Right. Well, Dad told her that Leland is an old friend of his, and he'd given him his credit card to go pick up some things for him at the store—'cause Leland doesn't get out in public."

"Doesn't he have servants for that?" Sam asked.

Lance chuckled, "That's exactly what your mother said. Dad explained that he'd been over at Leland's late at night. Rather than bother his staff, Leland just asked Dad to do it and bring it by the next day."

"So why did he still have the card?" Sam leaned her chin on her hand.

"Dad forgot to give it back, and Leland forgot to ask for it. So at the restaurant, Dad just accidentally pulled it out when he went to pay the bill."

"Oh," Samantha shrugged, satisfied with Geoffrey's explanation. "And Mom was still upset?"

"No, she wasn't upset. That seemed to satisfy her, but then Dad got all bent out of shape and wanted to know why she was looking at the bill in the first place. He accused her of meddling in his affairs. Got all defensive and the more he talked, the more irrational and irate he became."

"That seems odd," Samantha rubbed her chin.

"Well, it would be odd if it were anybody but my Dad. He's very private and if he thinks you're invading his privacy, he goes ballistic. He did that to Mom all the time . . . especially in that last year before she died."

"Wow, why is he like that?" Samantha pictured the cool, professional Geoffrey Nielson losing his stack. She decided he would make a formidable adversary.

Lance took a sip of soda before answering. "I don't know why he's like that, but he's gotten worse with age. And one word of caution if you ever have to deal with him—never, never question him about Leland Norris or his relationship with him. He's very defensive about Leland."

"Why?"

Lance leaned a little closer and lowered his voice. "I don't know. But I think Leland's got some kind of a hold on dad."

"Really?" Samantha leaned in, anxious to hear the story. "What kind of hold?"

"Well," Lance hesitated for a moment and appeared to be debating on whether to share what he knew. After a few moments he continued. "Dad and Leland were college roommates. Leland's always been a loner. He was an orphan, went through several foster homes and managed, out of sheer tenacity, to make a name for himself." Lance lowered his voice to a whisper and leaned his head closer to Samantha's, "Between you and me, he owns half of Savannah's construction operations. It's all buried in a web of corporations and subsidiaries, but Leland's behind them. What's more, most of the city contracts go through one of Leland's corporations."

"So you think your dad . . ." Samantha hesitated, unwilling to suggest that Lance's father could be involved in unethical business dealings.

Lance said what she was unwilling to vocalize, "I think Leland played a hand in not only Dad's sudden business success but also him being made City Manager."

"Why would Norris do that?" Samantha whispered.

"So that he could have a steady stream of government contracts." Lance lifted a single insinuative eyebrow.

Samantha leaned back against the booth, her eyes widened in surprise. Her mind whirled with the possibilities and the last words of her mother's journal ran through her mind. "*There's a concern at work over the government contracts, involves Geoffrey and Leland Norris. I've set up an appointment to talk with Sean Cooper about it tomorrow. Maybe he can help me figure it out. Sean was always a good young man. I know I can trust him."*

Samantha immediately remembered that she'd been so distracted with work and her date with Lance that she'd completely forgotten to call Sean. Now she'd have to wait until morning!

She was silent for several moments, collecting her thoughts. Lance cracked open another crab leg, letting her digest the information. She leaned closer toward Lance and whispered, "So you think there are unethical activities going on in the City Manager's office?"

Lance shrugged, "I really couldn't say, but I wouldn't put it past them."

"Wow," Samantha shook her head, still thrown by the information and especially the fact that her mother was dating someone involved in crooked politics. "Have you ever met Leland Norris? What's he like?"

"He came to our house several times when I was a teenager. He and dad had business dealings back then. He seemed like a nice guy, but I was just a kid. He'd hand me a twenty and ask me to wash his car." Lance chuckled. "What kid wouldn't be snowed over by something like that?"

"And since then?" she asked.

Lance finished chewing his food, then answered, "I haven't been around home enough to be there when he visits dad. I don't even know if he visits dad. He developed a bad phobia to crowds in the early 90's, even had to go through some therapy at one of those institutes. He's never been the same since. He stays in, has things delivered and runs his business from home."

"Interesting . . . and sad, really. I'd hate to live that way."

"Me too. I can't imagine never getting to go out to eat with a pretty girl," Lance winked playfully. Then, he took a deep breath and released it. "Okay, enough about reclusive millionaires and my power hungry father. Tell me about yourself. What do you like to do when you're not cooking delicious food?"

The discussion from there shifted into more typical first date conversation, but in the back of her mind Samantha couldn't let go of the information Lance had given her. Somehow it seemed significant, and she wanted to talk with Sean to find out how her mother fit into the picture.

Chapter 9

~ ✧ ~

Lance accompanied Samantha to her door. She opened her purse, retrieved her keys, then turned to face him, "Thanks, Lance. I had fun."

"Me too," he said.

Her keys clinked as she fiddled with them, "I'd ask you to come in, but I have to get up so early in the morning."

"I understand."

They looked into each other's eyes for a moment.

"Well, I better get going. I'll give you a call," he said, putting a hand on her shoulder.

"Okay," she nodded.

Lance leaned over and kissed her on the cheek, "Good night, Samantha."

She returned the sentiment, and he went to his car while she opened the door and stepped inside.

Samantha ran a hand through her blonde locks and yawned. She was tired. It had been a long day and as much as she enjoyed Lance's company she was glad he didn't want to come in. She was tired, and didn't feel up to entertaining anyone. As she flipped on the light, she thought about her evening with Lance. He was fun to be with, but she wasn't sure she wanted to pursue a relationship with him. She didn't know whether her hesitancy was caused by her usual fear of relationships or whether it was because Lance felt almost like a brother. Then again, maybe she wasn't being fair. Maybe she should give him a little more time.

"Instant chemistry only happens in the movies—right?" she mumbled to herself as she tossed her purse on the couch and went to the kitchen for a drink of water. She sipped it slowly and just as she prepared to go upstairs to bed, the phone rang.

"Sam?" asked a male voice.

"Yes."

"This is Sean Cooper. How're you doing?"

"Great," Samantha smiled and felt her pulse quicken a little. "You?"

"Busy," he replied. "Look, I know it's late. I hope I didn't wake you."

"You didn't," she assured him.

"I was wondering if you have to work tomorrow."

"Actually, I do. I go in at six, but I get off at noon."

"Any chance you'd care to spend the afternoon with me?"

Samantha felt her cheeks rise with her grin, "I'd love that, Sean."

"Great, what time works for you?"

"How about around one? That'll give me time to get home and change," she suggested.

"All right, I'll pick you up at your house," he said.

"Sounds good . . . oh, and Sean . . ." she began.

"Yes"

"I've been meaning to ask you about something. Mom was

supposed to have an appointment with you the day after she died. Do you know anything about that?" Samantha asked.

"Uh . . ." Sean's voice wavered a little, "You know, I only have a second here. We can talk tomorrow."

"All right," she said.

"Night, Sam. It's great having you back."

"Great to be back." She hung up the phone after he did and wondered about the sudden change in his voice. He didn't sound like he was in a hurry when he first called. Why the sudden rush to get off the phone?

~ ✧ ~

Samantha rose early for work, showered, dressed and went out to her car. At five, it was still dark outside. Just as she opened her car door, she felt a strong hand clamp her mouth and an arm go around her, binding her arms tightly against her sides. Fear seized Sam's mind and body. She screamed, but it wasn't loud enough for a neighbor to hear with the hand over her face. She struggled, stamping her heel into the man's foot. Before she could retaliate further, she heard a loud crack of metal hitting bone. The man's grip on her slackened, and he slipped with a thud to the concrete beside her.

Spinning around to see what had happened, Samantha saw Sean Cooper standing there, a pistol pointed at the man's unconscious body and a crowbar in his other hand.

"Sean!" she exclaimed and started toward him. He dropped the crowbar and put an arm around her pulling her protectively toward his body while he continued to watch the assailant.

"Are you all right?" he asked, his right arm still outstretched and pointing the pistol at the man's back.

She nodded that she was. "How? How did you get here? What's going on?"

"It's a long story. I'll explain later. First we need to get this guy to the authorities." He looked into her eyes, "Are you sure you're all right?"

Samantha nodded, her grateful eyes meeting his.

"Do you have some rope or something we can tie this guy up with until someone gets here?" Sean asked.

"I think there's some in the garage," she replied.

"Here," Sean held out the pistol. "Take this and keep it aimed at him while I go look."

"Oh, no," Sam shook her head nervously. "I'll go get the rope. You stay here and guard him."

"I'm not positive he was alone. I don't want to send you into the garage by yourself. You'll be safer here with the gun." Again, he motioned for her to take it.

"But what about you?" Samantha asked, still hesitating, then taking the weapon.

Sean reached down for the crowbar and lifted it from the pavement. "I'll be right back. Just stay here and keep that aimed at him. If he moves, shoot him in the leg or the arm . . . somewhere that won't kill him. He needs to be interrogated."

Samantha nodded, stood back from the man, and stretched the pistol out toward the body lying on the concrete. Her hands trembled as she kept her finger poised near the trigger.

"The garage door opener is hanging from the visor in my car," she told Sean. He went to her car, opened the door and pressed the button. As the door lifted he hurried toward the house and went into the garage. After several moments, Samantha saw the garage light turn on.

A few minutes later, Sean returned with a roll of duct tape. He pulled the man's hands behind his back and wrapped the tape around his wrists. Then he bound his legs with tape. Sean rolled Samantha's attacker over and she gasped at the sight.

"Do you know him?" Sean asked as his eyes met her frightened ones.

"No, no, it's just the blood." The man's head wound bled profusely, leaving a puddle of blood on the concrete where he lay. Sean felt for the man's pulse, and then lifted Samantha's keys off the pavement where they had fallen. He handed them to her, and she put them in her jacket pocket.

"He's still alive," Sean tore off another piece of tape and put it over the man's mouth. "Here, I'm going to need your help moving him out of the driveway."

"Where are we going to take him?" she asked, handing Sean the pistol. He shoved it into the inside pocket of his jacket.

"We'll put him on the porch and I'll call for help." Sean reached down and put a hand under each of the man's arms and motioned for Samantha to get the feet. She followed his instructions and they struggled to carry the rather large bald man to the porch. Once they'd set him down, Sean pulled a phone from his pocket and pressed a button.

"Go inside and round up enough clothes for a few days," he instructed.

Sam stopped and turned to him. "Why?"

"We need to get you somewhere safe," Sean said.

"I don't understand," she still stood there staring at him.

Sean held up a hand indicating that Sam should wait for his answer. "It's me," he said into the phone. "I need you over at Samantha Reynolds' right now. Yeah, thanks." He disconnected and slid the phone in his pocket.

"What's going on, Sean?" her eyes went from her old friend to the man lying on her porch. "Should we have moved him from the crime scene?"

"It's all right. I'll explain in the car. For now, I need you to pack up a few things so we can get out of here." He pointed toward the house, and she pulled the keys from her pocket.

She unlocked the door and they both stepped inside the house. Samantha flipped on an overhead light and asked, "Where are we going?"

"Somewhere safe. Pack enough clothes to last you three or four days." There was a sense of urgency in Sean's voice.

"Three or four days?" Samantha's voice lifted in protest. "I have work."

"You're going to have to call in sick or something," he stated in a matter-of-fact tone.

"I just got this job. I can't call in sick for that long," Samantha countered.

Sean took her by the shoulders and spoke directly to her, his blue eyes communicating the seriousness of the situation. "Your life is in danger, Sam. What's more important? Your life or a job?"

She tried to comprehend what was happening, but she

couldn't make sense of it. One thing she knew was she trusted Sean, and if he felt her life was in danger, she needed to listen to him. "Okay, all right," she relented.

He released her, and she hurried up the stairs to pack some clothes. When she returned, Sean was carrying Marjorie's computer out the door.

"What are you doing now?" she called after him.

"We're going to need this," he said. "Grab the keyboard, mouse and power cords."

Samantha set her suitcase down by the front door and went to her mother's study to get the computer parts. She handed them to Sean when he reentered the house.

"Why do we need the computer?" she asked.

"I need to search it and see if your mother recorded some information on it," Sean explained.

"Does this have anything to do with Leland Norris and Geoffrey Nielson?" Samantha asked.

Sean paused and his eyes met hers. She had obviously caught him off guard. He glanced at the man lying on the porch and shut the front door. "So you know?"

"I don't know anything really," she shrugged. "All I know is that Mom was going to speak to you about a connection between those two and something going on in the City Manager's office."

"She told you that?" his eyebrows lifted in surprise.

"In a manner of speaking."

"What's that supposed to mean?" Sean's gaze narrowed.

"Mom kept a journal."

"She kept a journal!" Sean exclaimed. "And you have it?"

"Yes," Samantha shrugged.

"Get it. We need that," he insisted.

"All right," she turned toward the stairs. "But I don't think it'll be that helpful. She really doesn't say that much."

"Get it anyway," he repeated.

"All right," she replied. Sean opened the front door and carried the computer equipment out to the car. When Samantha returned with the journal in hand, Sean was carrying her suitcase out to the car and a silver sedan was now parked alongside his in the driveway. She stood at the screen door watching.

Sean put her suitcase in the trunk and shut it. A man stepped out of the other car and approached Sean. They spoke for several moments and Sean pointed to the house.

The pair walked toward her. They lifted the unconscious man from the porch and carried him to the silver car. Sean seemed to be giving the man instructions and then he drove away.

"Who was that? Why didn't you call the police?" Samantha asked when Sean returned to the house.

"That's an undercover cop." He pointed his thumb over his shoulder, indicating the man who had left with her assailant. "Are you ready to go?"

"I guess. I need to call in to work though."

"You can do that on the way. Let's get going." He put his hand on her arm.

"Okay," Samantha locked the door and followed Sean

outside. He opened the passenger side for her and she got in.

When he slid behind the wheel, Samantha had her phone in her hand and was getting ready to call into work.

"Don't use your cell." He took the phone from her hand, rolled down the window, and tossed it out of the car. It cracked against the pavement and bounced into the grass.

"Why in the world did you do that?" she exclaimed. All this cloak and dagger stuff was really starting to get on her nerves.

"All cell phones have a GPS tracking system inside them. The last thing we need is these guys following us."

"Well you could have told me that while we were in the house! I could have left it there instead of you cracking it all over the pavement!" she shouted. "That was a top of the line phone."

"I'll buy you another one when this is all over." He handed her another cell phone, "Here, use this one."

"What's going on, Sean?" she asked for what felt like the hundredth time in the last fifteen minutes.

"They've tapped your home phone, and I don't know if they're tracking your cell phone, but we need to be careful." Sean started the engine.

Samantha met his gaze and a chill ran up her spine. "Someone's been monitoring my calls?"

"Yes," he said simply and backed out of the driveway.

"Who are they?" Samantha demanded.

"I'll explain everything in time," he assured. He pulled the car onto the street.

"How do you know that they aren't tapping your cell?" she wiggled his phone between her fingers.

"It's one of those prepaid ones. I picked it up yesterday. They don't even know I have it," he answered. "Go ahead and call into work so we have that out of the way."

"What am I going to tell them?" Her thumb hovered over the cell phone buttons.

"Tell them you've had a family emergency and have to leave town for a few days." He made a left turn.

Samantha didn't like the idea of lying to her employer, but she didn't seem to have a choice. First, she called Kay to ask her to cover for her for the next few days, and then she called the Ballastone and left a message for Mr. Salandi.

"I can call Travis later after he wakes up," she said as she set Sean's phone down in the cup holder at the front of his car.

Samantha watched Sean as he drove. He certainly wasn't the hesitant young man he'd been in youth. Every move he made now was decisive and authoritative. He'd changed significantly; for a split second she mourned the loss of her high school friend whose greatest worry was which rival he would be up against in the next basketball game.

But the sensation didn't last long for she was too fascinated by the man he'd become. She studied the dark stubble on his strong jaw line and his deep blue eyes that concentrated on the road.

"So are you going to tell me what's going on?" she prompted after several silent moments.

"Do you think you can hold out until we get where we're going? It'll only take about thirty minutes. Some of this is going to come as a shock, and I'd just feel more comfortable telling you when I'm not driving."

"A shock?"

Sean glanced at her as he nodded, and she noted the hint of dread in his sad blue eyes.

Chapter 10

~ ✧ ~

The next thirty minutes passed slowly for Samantha. Her mind whirled with questions she knew Sean wouldn't answer until they arrived at their destination. Making small talk about their lives seemed petty at this point, so the drive toward Tybee Island passed in silence. Samantha studied the greenery of the flat swampland through her window and thought of the dozens of questions she wanted to fire at Sean when they arrived wherever they were going.

"I always get a kick out of these turtle crossing signs," Sean pointed at a yellow sign with a turtle on it. "Anywhere else in the country you'd see deer or cattle crossing signs, but not here," Sean chuckled.

Samantha gave him an obligatory smile. Under less foreboding circumstances she would have found it humorous, but now she just wanted to get wherever they were going so she could find out what was going on.

Her hand rested on the leather seat between them. Sean reached over and put his hand over hers, and gave it a gentle squeeze. "Everything's going to be all right, Sam. I promise."

Her eyes met his reassuring ones, and she felt better. He looked back at the road, but laced his fingers with hers and continued to hold her hand as he drove.

His hand in hers made her feel secure and warm, and Samantha thought how much she'd missed him over the years. There were so many times when she wanted to pick up the phone and call him, to talk through the challenges of her life or just to celebrate her successes. But it seemed he was always involved with someone else at those times, and she didn't dare encroach upon his life. She'd turned to her mother instead, and they'd grown even closer as a result. It seemed only fitting now that her mother wasn't here for her, Sean would be.

"I sure have missed you," his voice was lower than usual as his eyes locked with hers. Samantha could feel the warmth settle in her chest; then he looked back at the road.

"I was just thinking the same thing about you," her soft reply betrayed her emotions.

He lifted her hand to his lips and kissed the back of it. Then he placed it back on the seat, released it and used both hands to drive. He turned down a dirt road that was sparsely covered with gravel. It seemed to take forever for Sean's car to maneuver around potholes and ease over jarring bumps.

After about a half of a mile, they pulled in front of a small beach house set a couple hundred yards from a dock that descended to a small private beach.

"Is this your place?" she asked as Sean pulled his car into the garage and grabbed his cell phone from the cup-holder.

"No, it's a friend's. Nobody should find us here." He got out of the car, lifted a rock and retrieved a garage door opener. He pressed the button and the door lifted. Sean returned to the car, pulled the car into the garage and turned off the engine. They both got out, and Samantha joined Sean by the trunk. He grabbed her suitcase and his duffle bag, and she gathered up her mother's keyboard, mouse and power cords.

Sean went to the door that connected the garage to the interior of the house, pressed a button to close the garage and stuck his key in the door. The garage went dark, and Sam put her hand on Sean's back, assuring herself of his presence. In a moment, he'd unlocked the door, and they stepped inside the kitchen. Samantha's eyes went from the black and white checkered tile to the white cabinets and steel appliances.

"There's an office down the hall," he pointed to a corridor to their right. "We can set up the computer in there."

Samantha went in the direction he'd pointed, and Sean set down their bags on the kitchen floor. She stepped into the well-lit office that overlooked the ocean. It was a cozy room, lined with oak bookshelves and matching filing cabinets. Samantha set the computer accessories down on the oak desk in the center of the room and walked toward the large window that spanned nearly the entire far wall. She stood there admiring the incredible view until Sean entered, carrying the CPU under one arm and the flat panel monitor in his other hand.

He set them both on the desk and joined her by the window.

"It's so beautiful, isn't it?" she observed.

"Incredibly beautiful," he agreed, but he didn't look at the view; his eyes were fixed on Samantha.

She could feel the warmth of his gaze on her face and a blush crept involuntarily to her cheeks. "So," she turned abruptly toward him. "You promised to tell me what's going on once we got here."

His expression darkened and his head lowered, "Come on in here where we can sit down, and I'll tell you everything."

She followed him out of the office, down the corridor. Only a bar separated the kitchen from the great room. The house was an A-frame with a high vaulted ceiling and a rock fireplace that ascended the full height of the wall.

Sean took a seat on a tan leather couch and motioned for her to join him. She sat down on the opposite end and shifted to face him. He turned toward her, removed his windbreaker and draped it over his knee that was propped on the couch.

He rolled up the sleeves of his green Oxford and leaned an arm across the back of the couch. He looked as if he were trying to get comfortable, but instantly gave up and rose to his feet. Samantha's eyes followed him as he came to stand in front of her. She shifted to face him, putting both feet on the floor and waiting for him to begin.

"Sam, I don't know how to tell you this," he stuck his hands in his jean pockets, turned his back to her and paced away a few steps. He turned back toward her, then came to stand directly in front of her and squatted down. Taking her hands in his, he looked into her face, and she could see the moisture brimming in his eyes.

"Sam, your mom was murdered."

"What?" Samantha's mouth dropped open. Her mind whirled, trying to fit the pieces together. Tears filled her eyes as she searched Sean's face. Was he serious? Of course he was. He wouldn't make up something like this! "Why? . . . How?" she stammered.

"We believe she was killed because she knew too much about

illegal activities in the City Manager's office," Sean said.

"They said it was a heart attack. How could it be murder?" she shook her head negatively.

"It was murder, made to look like a heart attack," he clarified.

"How is that possible?" Sam's heart raced and she felt as if all the blood had drained from her face.

"An injection of potassium chloride will induce a heart attack," Sean explained.

"But wouldn't it have shown up in the autopsy? Wouldn't it have left traces? The doctors never mentioned anything about this," she reasoned. Her mother dying of a heart attack at such a young age had been difficult enough to comprehend, but murder?

He rose to his feet and paced a little. "It doesn't leave any traces. It's the perfect instrument to commit the perfect murder. And you don't have to be a doctor to get hold of it. Heck, the stuff is more soluble than table salt and anyone can order it off the net for a few dollars. Injection needles aren't that hard to come by."

"How do you know that's what it was if there were no traces? How can you be sure?" She stared up at him.

"Think about it, Sam." He sat down close to her on the couch facing her. "Your mother never had a heart problem." Sean counted the points on his fingers. "She had no history of any kind of heart abnormality and then suddenly she suffers a massive coronary in the middle of the night. It just doesn't add up."

"I've thought a heart attack was unusual myself, but murder?

That's quite a leap isn't it?" Samantha protested.

"My friend in the DA's office helped me check further into the autopsy. They did find a small needle mark in Marjorie's arm where she'd evidently been injected with something. There's no record of her having been to the doctor recently or giving blood. We believe someone injected her with potassium chloride, and it caused a massive heart attack."

"But who? Why?" Samantha's blonde locks swayed as she shook her head side-to-side.

"Your mother called me the night she died and told me that she suspected that Geoffrey Nielson and Leland Norris were running some kind of scam in the City Manager's office. She said that Geoffrey was accepting inflated bids that Norris made on projects. She claimed there were other contractors making better offers, but Geoffrey wasn't accepting them."

He leaned his hand on the couch and continued, "I told her it wasn't uncommon for the city not to accept the lowest bid because a low bid usually means poor quality. But she insisted that Norris' bids were always the highest and were always accepted. She also had reason to believe they were cutting corners on the projects and not performing up to spec. She wanted to talk with me about it the next day, and we set up an appointment. But, of course, she never arrived."

"Are you saying you think either Geoffrey Nielson or Leland Norris had my mother murdered?" Samantha's voice lifted with surprise.

"One or both of them," Sean replied. "Geoffrey could have easily done it himself. He had no trouble gaining access to her house."

Samantha leaned toward Sean and whispered, "But how did they find out about the appointment? How did they know she was on to them?" The thought occurred to Samantha that someone could be listening to their conversation at this very moment. Who was to say they hadn't bugged this place or her purse or something else?

"That's just it." Sean answered. "The only way they could have known was that they had her phone tapped. Either that or my secretary was eavesdropping. But she's an older woman—the mother of a friend of mine that I've known for years—and it just doesn't make sense that it would be her. After what happened to you this morning, I'm convinced Marjorie's phones are tapped. Remember, last night you mentioned that you knew something about your mother setting the appointment with me. You also told me your work hours."

"So you think they were listening and that's why someone was thereto abduct me this morning?" Samantha asked.

"I don't think they were just going to abduct you." There was a grave expression on his face. "I think they were going to kill you."

Samantha gulped, realizing that Sean was probably right. "But you were there to save me." She put a hand over his where it rested on the couch.

"I had a feeling the line was tapped. After what you said on the phone, I had to make sure you were safe." He covered her hand with his other one.

"How long were you outside my house?" she asked.

"I came right over after we got off the phone. I didn't want to take any chances," Sean answered.

"Thank you, Sean. No wonder you look so exhausted." Her eyes held both gratitude and sympathy.

"I called my friend in the DA's office and asked him to have someone ready just in case anything happened. I couldn't justify calling the police right away because all of this is just a theory . . . or at least it was a theory until this morning. I think the attack on you proves something." Sean looked toward the fireplace, pondering for a moment. "If they can just get something out of that guy who attacked you."

"So they're interrogating him now?"

"I hope so," he nodded, meeting her gaze once more.

"Wouldn't the police have wanted to interrogate us? Why didn't we just go to the police department? We would have been safe there," Samantha reasoned.

"Well, we probably should have, but I just know the answer is somewhere in Marjorie's things and I think we're in a better position to find the answer," Sean explained. "The police still aren't convinced that I'm right about your mother's murder. They say I don't have enough evidence."

"Did you check into Mom's findings? Is the city giving too many contracts to Leland Norris?" Samantha asked.

"I called my friend at the DA's office and he wasn't convinced at first. I guess he just humored me because we are old friends from college. But as he began investigating, he found what Marjorie found. Leland Norris has set up dozens of companies and corporations in different names so they can't be easily traced back to him. We know he went to college with Geoffrey Nielson, but we can't find any reason for Geoffrey to be helping Norris other than friendship."

"That's not enough?" Samantha asked.

"Nobody in Nielson's position is going to risk his job just to send his old friend a bunch of contracts. There's something else going on here." Sean raked a hand through his hair and let it flop on the back of the couch. "But we can't find any evidence of blackmail or even where Nielson's received any kickbacks from Norris."

Samantha's eyes brightened suddenly, realizing she knew something that might help. "I had dinner with his son Lance last night, and he told me Geoffrey and Leland used to be business partners. Maybe Geoffrey still owns some of those businesses with Norris?"

"You're seeing Lance Nielson?" A wave of irritation washed over Sean's face.

"I'm not 'seeing' him, Sean. It was just dinner and a movie."

"Still, this guy could be dangerous. His father could have murdered your mother."

"Lance isn't dangerous. He's too laid back to be dangerous," Samantha reasoned.

"So you know him that well? You've been seeing him long enough to know he can be trusted?" Sean released her hand, and she thought she saw hurt mingled with the anger in his eyes.

Samantha released a nervous giggle, "You're jealous."

Sean stood up and started pacing around the room. "I'm just concerned for your safety, Sam. First your mother is murdered—most likely by Geoffrey or one of his men—and then his son starts befriending you—probably to find out how much you know so he can report back to dear old dad."

"It wasn't like that. Lance didn't get any information out of me. If anything, he told me quite a bit that I think we can use. I don't think he has a clue that his father could be involved in murder, or he never would have told me what he did."

"So what exactly did he tell you?" Sean folded his arms across his chest and stared down at her almost as if he were daring her to provide something useful in Lance's comments.

Samantha's lips curled up into a faint smile. There was something adorable about Sean Cooper when he got this way. She recalled a few other times when he became this bullheaded, and each time it had been when she was dating someone. She'd been too young and naive as a teenager to realize it, but it was jealousy then, and it was jealousy now.

"Lance doesn't get along with his father. He calls him power hungry. He insinuated that Geoffrey and Leland Norris were involved in something unethical and said he'd overheard an argument between Mom and Geoffrey that connected the two men."

"Really? What was the argument about?" Sean relaxed his arms and let his hands fall to his sides.

"Evidently Geoffrey paid for a meal with one of Leland Norris' personal credit cards. My mom questioned him about it, and he claimed that Norris had given him the card, asked him to pick something up for him, and then he forgot to give it back."

"And Marjorie didn't buy that?" Sean asked.

"Lance said it wasn't that Mom didn't believe him, it was that Geoffrey suddenly became irate and yelled at her for prying into his business. She'd looked at the dinner receipt when

Geoffrey went to the restroom, so he accused her of spying." Samantha paused for a moment, then asked, "Do you think she was spying? Do you think she'd already figured out about the contracts and that was why she was dating Geoffrey in the first place?"

"I don't know," Sean shrugged, turned and paced toward the fireplace with his back to her. "If it was the reason she dated him, she was one brave woman." He sighed, "Or incredibly stupid, depending upon how you look at it."

"My mother wasn't stupid," Samantha defended.

Sean turned toward her, an apologetic expression on his face, "I know. I would just hope that if she knew about it for that long she would have come to me for help. Surely she should have known she could trust me." Sean rubbed his tired eyes. "I just wish she would have come to me sooner. Or if I'd just seen what Geoffrey was doing, maybe your mom would be alive right now. I should have seen it coming . . ." He let his hand drop to his side in frustration, a dejected expression capturing his handsome face.

Samantha rose from the couch and went to him. She put her hands on his shoulders and looked up into his eyes. "It's not your fault, Sean. Mom trusted you. She said as much in her journal. She evidently didn't realize how deeply in danger she was."

He put his hands to her waist and then pulled her into his embrace. Hugging her tightly against him he whispered into her ear, "I'm so sorry, Sam . . . so sorry." She closed her eyes and rested her head on his shoulder, nuzzling into the crook of his neck, inhaling the remnant scent of yesterday's cologne. Sean let his palm rest softly against her cheek, his fingers sifting through her blonde hair. When Samantha lifted her eyes to his, Sean's thumb brushed at the lingering teardrop on her cheek. "Are you going to be all right?" he asked.

She nodded her head, but her pulse accelerated, pounding in her chest. Warmth drizzled throughout her body emanating from the point of his touch. She felt dizzy, light-headed with anticipation as Sean's gaze lowered to her lips and his head drew even closer to her own. His mouth hovered above her lips as his gaze held hers.

His eyes seemed to feast upon the form, features and textures of her face with an adoration she'd never seen in a man. When his attention fell to where his thumb traced the contours of her lips, the intensity of the moment sent Samantha's emotions flying in a dozen directions.

"Sean," she breathed, taking his face in her hands, her palms resting on the dark stubble of his cheeks. She pulled him closer until his mouth captured hers. The initial tender meeting of their lips quickly became intense and fiery. Suddenly everything made sense as if her entire life culminated in this moment. Being in Sean's arms was as familiar as coming home, yet simultaneously as thrilling as the intriguing mystery they were trying to solve.

His cell phone rang three times before Sean pulled himself away from her. Sliding it from his pocket, he stepped back to answer it.

Chapter 11

~ ✧ ~

"Hello," Sean bent his head down, staring at his white tennis shoes with his cell phone pressed to his ear. "Yeah, we're here . . . we still need to go through Marjorie's computer and journal." He glanced up at Samantha who watched him. "I've just been bringing Samantha up to speed on what's happening."

A slight smile tugged at Sean's lips, and then he turned his back to her and took a few steps away. "Yeah, I'll call you as soon as we find anything . . . okay . . . bye."

"Who was that?" Samantha inquired as Sean stuffed the phone in the pocket of his jeans.

"That was Paul Jackson, my friend in the DA's office. He just wanted to know if we'd found any evidence yet." He turned back toward her and motioned for her to follow him. "We need to get busy and see what we can find in your mom's computer and journal." He went down the hall toward the office. Samantha grabbed her purse from the couch and followed him.

When she stepped inside the office, she put her purse on the desk and pulled out her mother's journal. "I've already looked through this, and I don't think there is much here that's going to help."

She set it on the desk while Sean hooked up Marjorie's

computer. "Maybe I should read it. A fresh set of eyes might find something you missed." He looked up at her from where he knelt on the floor, plugging in the equipment.

Samantha's mind shot back to the entries in the journal about herself. She didn't want Sean reading about her breakup with Jerry or her mother's worries about her becoming socially withdrawn.

Once the system booted, he pulled out a chair and gestured for Samantha to take the seat in front of the computer, "Look through your mom's files and see if you see anything that looks legal or has to do with Geoffrey or Leland Norris."

"Okay," she nodded and sat down.

"While you're looking, I'll go through this," he reached for the journal, and Samantha instinctively put her hand over his to stop him.

"Really, Sean, there's nothing useful in there," her green eyes pled with him. The journal was just too embarrassing.

"You might have missed something . . . there might have been something you didn't realize applied at the time you read it," he reasoned.

"Please, Sean," she tightened her hand on his.

"What's wrong, Sam? I promise, anything personal stays private."

Samantha's shoulders slumped as she exhaled, "Look, there's personal stuff in there about me. It's all highly exaggerated. Mom was such a worrywart—it was really never that bad. I just . . . just . . . don't feel comfortable with you reading it."

Sean smiled sympathetically. "Then anything I find in there

about you, I'll just take with a grain of salt and skim over, but we really need to cover every base."

Samantha released an exasperated sigh and removed her hand from his, "Okay, but before you're tempted to believe anything you read about me, I get to tell my side of the story."

"Fair enough," he winked, lifted the journal, and sat in the chair beside her.

For the next twenty minutes, Sean read and Samantha searched through the files on the computer.

Sean chuckled, "Your mother really was a worrywart."

"What did you find?" Samantha looked at him.

"She'd just about resigned you to life in a nunnery, hadn't she? Were you really having this hard of a time getting out?" he asked.

Samantha shrugged, "I don't know. I just didn't want to date in Atlanta after we broke up. It seemed like everywhere I went was somewhere I'd gone with Jerry."

"You really loved him then?" Sean had a mixed expression on his face—as if he were trying to decide whether to be jealous or break Jerry's arm for hurting her.

"I thought I did." She turned her attention to scanning the files on Marjorie's computer. "But I'm over him now."

"What about Lance?" Sean prodded.

Samantha didn't register his question. Instead she opened a picture on Marjorie's computer, "Here, look at this."

Sean scooted closer so he could see. "That's Marjorie and Geoffrey on his yacht."

"There's a whole folder full of these." She pointed at the

screen and then clicked the mouse to open the folder. Samantha pulled up a dozen different photos of her mother and Geoffrey in different settings. "They did look good together," she muttered.

"Your mother made anyone look good," Sean replied, "even a scum ball like Geoffrey Nielson."

"I'll keep looking and see what else I can find," she said, and Sean returned to reading the journal. Another fifteen minutes passed as they each studied their tasks.

"Wait a minute," Samantha exclaimed, her heart racing with her latest find. "I think I've got something here!"

"What?" Sean's blue eyes darted toward the monitor.

"I decided to search by date. There's a file here called *insurance.doc* last updated the night she died, and it's password protected."

"Do you have any idea what the password could be?" He scooted his chair closer to hers and leaned toward the computer.

"I know a few things Mom used. I'll try those." Samantha entered a combination of family names and birthdates, but nothing worked. Frustrated after dozens of attempts, she ran her hands through her hair and shoved her swivel chair away from the keyboard. "I don't know, Sean. I just don't know." She inhaled and released a heavy sigh.

Sean set the journal on the desk and rose to his feet. He stood behind her and began massaging her shoulders in an effort to relieve some of her tension. Samantha leaned back and closed her eyes.

After a few minutes, she remembered something, "Wait. I

have an idea!" She moved closer to the keyboard once more. "I don't know if this is it, but it might be. It's an older password she used. Samantha typed, *MST2k1c* and pressed the Enter button. "We're in!" she exclaimed.

"How did you remember that?" Sean asked, leaning over her shoulder to look at the keyboard.

"Marjorie, Samantha, Travis, 2 kids, 1 cat," Samantha explained.

"Oh, man! Look at that!" Sean's eyes widened as he saw what came up on the screen.

Samantha scrolled through the document, "This is a log of everything she had on Geoffrey and Leland Norris!"

"Print it," Sean urged.

Samantha sent it to the printer and continued to read the screen.

"Looks like by November she'd researched the companies with government contracts," Sean observed. "She's got the genealogy of the main ones here. Anderson Construction is owned by Savannah Construction, Inc. which is owned by Emerald Inc., which is a subsidiary of Leland Enterprises."

"Then there's this Savannah Remodeling Experts owned by Riverfront Construction, a subsidiary of Universal Construction which is owned by Leland Enterprises," Samantha added.

Sean gestured toward the screen. "Leland's really got these projects buried deep. Your mom was one sharp woman to figure this out."

"She was good at her job. Always very thorough," Samantha replied. "Looks like she's documented what Lance told me here too—about her seeing Geoffrey use one of Leland Norris' credit cards."

"And that led her to searching deeds and documents for Leland's signature," Sean added. "Just look at this! She's scanned the original documents!"

"These signatures don't match," Samantha observed. "Look at this one of Norris' from the early 90's. It doesn't match the recent ones."

"Your mother's pointed out here that the N in Nielson looks a lot like the N in Norris. She thought they were the same man, but we know that Nielson and Norris went to college together so that's not it."

"Keep reading," Samantha urged excitedly. "She thinks that Geoffrey has assumed Norris' identity! Read this entry on page 15:

> "December 22nd. I think the incident the other night has blown over, and Geoffrey trusts me again. He called to apologize for what happened, and I invited him over for dinner and a movie. My mind has been spinning with the possibilities. What if Geoffrey has assumed Norris' identity? I had to find out and there was only one way for me to do it.
>
> I know it was dangerous, but I found a mild sedative my doctor gave me when my back went out last April. I slipped it into his soup, and when we settled on the couch to watch the movie, he fell asleep with his head on my lap. Fortunately he was

lying on his side so he could see the TV, and I pulled his wallet from his back pocket.

At first I didn't see anything—not even Leland's credit card from the other night, but then I found a zippered compartment. Inside it was a couple credit cards in Leland's name and a driver's license with Geoffrey's picture, but Leland's name on it!

I was so scared that I could barely stop my hands from shaking long enough to slip the wallet back in his back pocket! Then I had to wait there with his head on my lap until he awakened. I've never been so terrified in my life! Finally he woke up and it took everything I could muster to kiss him goodnight. But I think I acted well enough. He didn't seem to be suspicious.

I hate to say it . . . to actually write it here . . . but I think Geoffrey killed Leland, assumed his identity and has been funneling government projects through a web of corporations designed to hide the fact that he is benefitting from the over-inflated contracts!"

"Wow," Sean whispered. "This is big!" He began pacing around the room, sifting through the pages that had come off the printer. "If she's right, then Geoffrey probably murdered Leland Norris when they were business partners, took over his identity, built this web of sub-corporations and has been funneling government projects through to his corporations for nearly a decade!"

Samantha leaned her elbows on the desk in front of her and rested her head on her hands. "I can't believe she put herself in this kind of danger! Why didn't she go directly to the police?" Tears misted Samantha's vision, and she squeezed her eyes shut. "Why couldn't I sense she was in trouble when I saw her over Christmas?"

Sean set the stack of paper on the desk and stepped behind it to join Samantha. He put his hands on her shoulders and leaned over to kiss her cheek. "It's not your fault, Sam. There's no way you could have known."

Samantha rubbed her eyes, "I know. I just can't help but think she would be alive right now if she'd never met him, if she'd never started looking into all this."

Sean squatted down beside her and turned her chair to face him. Looking intently into her misty eyes he assured, "Your mother was a brave woman, a great lady. Geoffrey Nielson will pay for what he did to her. I promise you that." He reached into his pocket and retrieved a memory stick. "Put the file on this. I'll get it to Paul so he can get it to the police immediately."

She took the memory stick, placed it in the USB port and copied the file. "Do you need me to write down the password or can you remember it?"

"I think I can remember it—MST2k1c—right?" he said.

"Right," she replied, nodding her head as she worked on the computer.

Sean stood up when she handed him the memory stick. He put it in his pocket and retrieved his cell phone to call Paul.

"Paul, it's Sean. We've found something on the computer

that you need to see." He paused, listening to his friend. Samantha stood up and went to the window, staring out at the ocean. She tried to calm her nerves by taking deep breaths, but the thought of what had happened to her mother made her feel sick to her stomach.

"No, I'd rather not talk about it over the phone," she heard Sean say. "Let's meet in person. How about Fort Pulaski? It's not very busy this time of year. Meet me just inside by the first set of barracks . . . Okay . . . around ten. See ya." Sean disconnected the call and walked toward the window where Samantha still stood with her gaze fixed on the ocean.

He put his hand on her shoulder, "Are you all right?"

"Yeah," she nodded, still staring numbly at the waves crashing onto the shoreline.

"Look at me," he whispered, gently turning her toward him. Her eyes met his for only a flickering instant before she slid her arms around his waist and nestled her head on his shoulder. His hand rubbed her back consolingly. "It's going to be all right. We'll get this guy."

"Thank you," she replied. "For being here for me . . . for . . . for saving my life."

He put his hand to her cheek, raising her gaze to meet his, "Just promise me one thing." Her eyes searched the earnest expression on his face as he continued, "Promise me you'll never walk out of my life again."

His request was the only desire of her heart—to be with him, to be his. She'd begun to realize that her relationship with Jerry was just her settling for less than she wanted. At the time, Sean was considering marriage himself. Assuming he was unattainable, she'd plunged headlong into marriage plans with Jerry. But she hadn't truly loved him. Sean was the only man she'd ever loved. She knew that now as she looked up into his questioning eyes. He still awaited her reply.

"I'm not going anywhere," she whispered just before his lips met hers. She put her hands on his strong jaws, feeling the stubble on his cheeks as his mouth worked a passionate spell upon her senses. His kiss vanquished every worry or consideration from her mind. In his embrace she found the piece of her life that was missing, an assuring wholeness that she had only tasted once before this day—as a young woman too foolish to recognize it.

Sam did not know how many minutes passed before Sean ended the blissful reprieve he had given her. He stepped back, leaving only a lingering hand to her cheek. "I've got to get ready to go."

"I'm going with you," she replied.

"No, you stay here where I know you'll be safe. No one knows we're here—not even Paul—not even my friend who owns the place. I'll meet Paul at Fort Pulaski, give him the file, and you hide the printout somewhere it'll be safe. Then I'll come back here, and we'll wait until Geoffrey's taken into custody."

Sean leaned over the desk, grabbed a pen and a post-it note and started writing. She watched over his shoulder as he wrote down three phone numbers.

He handed it to her, "This is my cell number, Paul Jackson's cell and then the third number belongs to David Evans. He's the undercover cop who's been helping us. If anything goes wrong, call David. He'll know what to do."

Samantha briskly approached him, putting her hands on his shoulders, "What do you mean, if anything goes wrong? Is meeting Paul dangerous?"

"No, no," he insisted. "I just want to make sure we cover every contingency."

Samantha nodded her understanding and slipped the paper into her pocket.

Sean glanced at his watch. "I need to go now." He stuck his hand in his pocket assuring that he still had the memory stick. Then he retrieved a second phone from his pocket and handed it to her. "Use this if you need to reach me. I won't be gone long. I'll just meet Paul at Fort Pulaski, give him the stick, fill him in on our findings and come right back here."

Samantha accompanied him to the door. He kissed her, stepped into the garage and raised the door. "Close the garage and lock up good once I leave."

"Be careful, Sean."

"I will," his eyes met hers and then he got into his car.

Samantha closed the garage after he left and double checked all the doors to ensure that they were locked and double bolted. All she could do now was wait.

Chapter 12

~ ✧ ~

All the way to Fort Pulaski, Sean had difficulty keeping his mind on the circumstances at hand. He kept thinking about Samantha and the way she made him feel. How could he have ever let her go all those years ago? Then again, letting her pursue her dreams was the right thing to do.

The problem was that since then she had never been available when he was. To think he'd almost made the mistake of his life and married Ellen Harrison! She'd turned out to be a manipulative wench, just out for status as the wife of an up-and-coming politician. She'd pushed him to seek political offices he had no desire to obtain. He was satisfied being an Alderman on the city council. But Ellen wanted him to run for mayor, eventually even governor. She pushed so hard that Sean finally broke down and told her he had no intentions for high government office. That was the end of their relationship.

Rather than being heartbroken, Sean felt as if a weight had been lifted from his shoulders. He felt freer than he had in the previous three years—ever since he'd started dating Ellen. Since the break-up he'd enjoyed his freedom and remained aloof from women.

Now, into his life walks the only woman he'd ever truly cared for. It was truly amazing that these sad and sinister events could lead him to such a fortuitous place, with Samantha Reynolds back in his life.

His thoughts kept his mind so occupied that he almost missed the turn to Fort Pulaski, but he noticed it in time and turned right. He stopped at the gate and paid to enter, then parked his car.

He got out and walked toward the entrance. He passed an oak tree that had a limb jutting out parallel to the ground, nearly as long as the tree itself was high. It was a strange looking phenomenon, like an arm reaching out from the base of the trunk. Even though he'd been to the fort before, he couldn't help but marvel again at the unusual tree. He passed it and started toward the visitor's center, then turned toward the fort leaving the visitor's center behind him. He proceeded down the side-walk. Immaculately manicured green lawns and rolling hills surrounding him. A moat ran along the sidewalk to his left straight toward the fort entrance. He passed a palm tree and the sidewalk veered left. He followed it around, turning right and crossed the drawbridge that spanned the moat into the red brick fort.

Once he reached the interior of the structure, he turned left and proceeded until he saw the barred barracks along the perimeter. Paul wasn't there yet. Sean checked his watch. It was five past ten. His eyes scanned the interior of the fort. The center was an open lawn and the enclosed walls of the fort were a series of archways. Cannons were placed atop the walls.

Sean's gaze traveled from one archway to the next searching for Paul, just in case he'd gone to the wrong place. He saw no one. Assuming Paul was just running late, he turned his attention toward the barracks and looked inside. He studied the wooden floor, the white paint-chipped bunks, and the timeworn bricks comprising the walls. Just as he thought about what it would be like to be a soldier during the Revolutionary War and reside in such a place, he felt a searing pain on the back of his head and slipped to the ground, unconscious.

It had been nearly three hours since Sean left. Samantha hadn't heard a word from him or Paul in all that time. She paced around the great room trying to decide what she should do. She'd already tried to call Sean twice from the cell phone he'd left her. She'd just about decided to call Officer Evans when the cell phone rang.

It was Sean's cell number. She rushed to answer it, "Sean, are you all right? Where are you?"

But the voice on the other end wasn't Sean's. "Miss Reynolds," the man said.

"Yes," came her tentative reply.

"If you ever want to see Sean Cooper alive, you'll do exactly what I say."

Samantha's pulse raced. Her worst fears had become reality. Her hand trembled as she held the phone to her ear. "Who is this? What have you done with Sean?"

"Bring me Marjorie's computer and journal, and I'll let Mr. Cooper go."

"Put Sean on the phone! I want to know he's all right."

After a few moments of silence, Samantha heard Sean's

voice, "It's a trap, Sam! Don't do it!"

She heard a loud crack and a groan. "Sean! Sean, are you all right?"

"Are you listening to me, Miss Reynolds? Do I have your attention?" the male voice continued.

"Yes," she swiped the back of her hand to her cheek, wiping away her tears.

"Good. Come alone or he dies. Bring Marjorie's computer and journal to Fort Pulaski. Go to just outside the drawbridge and wait. You have one hour or he's dead."

"Wait!" she cried, but the call disconnected. She didn't even have a way to get there! She had no car. Her mind leapt frantically, unable to settle upon what to do next, then she remembered she had Officer Evan's number. She reached in her pocket, retrieved the number and dialed it. Fortunately, he answered and said he'd be there within thirty minutes.

Samantha gathered her mother's computer and journal and set them by the front door, ready and waiting for David Evans' arrival. She sat on the couch and buried her head in her hands, fighting to keep her wits about her. All she could think to do was pray . . . pray for Sean's safety and that they could get there in time to save his life.

She waited by the door when David Evans' familiar silver sedan pulled into the drive. He stepped out, his firearm drawn as he approached the house. She saw him pull his shield out as he approached the door. He held it up, "Miss Reynolds. It's me, Officer Evans. I'm here to take you to Fort Pulaski."

Sam opened the door and let him in. "The kidnapper wants

the computer and the journal," she said as she picked up the journal and the officer holstered his gun and took the computer. "We need to hurry. We only have about thirty minutes before he'll kill Sean."

They got in the car and the officer started backing out of the driveway, "Any idea who has him?" he asked.

"The voice sounded disguised, but I'm almost positive it was Geoffrey Nielson. The evidence we found on my mom's computer indicates that he killed Leland Norris, assumed his identity and killed my mother when she figured out what he'd done."

The officer's eyebrows rose in surprise. "And how did they get Sean?"

"He went there to meet Paul to give him some evidence. That was over three hours ago."

"Have you heard from Paul?"

"No, he's not answering his cell. I tried to call him when I couldn't get Sean."

"Then we have to assume Nielson has him too."

"I suppose so." Samantha sat there wringing her hands.

"Okay, we need to figure out a plan," the officer suggested. "First, I'm calling for backup."

"They said I had to come alone," she reminded him.

"Well, I'm not sending you in there alone. We'll make it look like you're alone, but I'll be close by protecting you." The officer radioed dispatch and requested a SWAT team to meet him at Fort Pulaski. They were to come in unmarked cars and be ready to take his instructions when they arrived.

It took about twenty minutes to get to the road to the fort. Officer Evans pulled over to the side of the freeway, opened the trunk and started to climb in.

"Drive into the fort, park and then come open the trunk. Take the computer and journal and walk slowly toward the building. Leave the trunk ajar, and I'll get out and be right behind you," Officer Evans instructed.

Samantha shut the officer into the trunk and got behind the wheel. Her pulse raced as she turned down the road, paid at the gate and drove toward the parking lot. She parked the car and opened the trunk, then took out the computer and journal.

"Remember, walk slowly. I'll not let you out of my sight. You're going to be just fine," he assured.

Samantha carried the computer under one arm and the journal in her other hand as she walked past the strange tree, past the visitor's center, and down the long straight sidewalk toward the fort.

Then she turned left and noticed a cement bunker cut into a grass-covered mound beside her. The moat and drawbridge lay to her right. The bunker was taped off for maintenance, and she recognized this location as where she was supposed to wait. She stood there for several moments facing the entrance and praying that Sean was still alive.

She gasped when she felt the hard steel of a gun barrel pointed in her side. "Be quiet and come with me. One word and you're dead," a male voice whispered gruffly in her ear, his rancid cigar breath puffing against her hair. He yanked her backwards toward the bunker, and then made her deliver the computer and journal to another burly man on the other side of the tape. "Get inside," he ordered, shoving her to the ground. Samantha quickly crawled under the tape.

The man joined her on the other side and rammed his pistol into her back. He urged her forward a few feet until they were no longer visible from the entrance. At that point, he slammed her against a concrete wall. Normally, she would have cried out, but she dared not make a sound lest the villain fire his weapon. The goon pulled her hands behind her back, handcuffed her wrists and tied a gag around her mouth.

Yanking her by the arm, he told her to start moving again and took her deeper into the underground bunker. Samantha remembered the bunkers at Fort Pulaski were once used to store ammunition, but now it was just a series of cement tunnels and rooms. The man nudged her onward until they came to a lighted area where a card table stood to her right. There was a notebook computer setting on it with some sort of portable power supply. To her left sat two men bound and gagged, sitting with their backs to the cement wall. She could barely make out in the shadows that one man appeared to be completely unconscious. The other's head was moving. At the table sat Geoffrey Nielson staring at the computer monitor. A small lamp on the table was all that lit the cavern

As Samantha drew closer she recognized the conscious man as Sean. Dried blood matted to the left side of his head and a trail of dark red blood dried in a rivulet down the side of his face.

She tried to say his name through the cloth, but it only came out as a moan. Sean's eyes quickly darted toward her and he shifted, evidently trying to reach her, but his hands were cuffed behind his back and his feet were tied together. Their eyes met and hers misted instantly for now she saw just how badly he'd been beaten. His eye was black and not only was there dried blood from his head wound, but his face had a large laceration across his cheekbone.

Geoffrey ordered the man carrying the computer to set it down on the table. Then, he hooked it up to his notebook computer while the man guarding her shoved her on the ground next to Sean. She fell down hard, her tailbone slamming into the cold concrete. She winced as he roughly pulled her feet straight out in front of her and tied them with a rope.

When the man moved out of her way, Sam noticed that Sean's memory stick lay on the card table. From the speed at which Geoffrey located the file on Marjorie's computer, she deduced he'd already read the memory stick.

"What's the password?" Geoffrey stared at Samantha. He nodded at her guard who pulled down her gag.

"What's the password?" he repeated.

"I'm not telling you anything. You said you'd let Sean go if I brought you the computer and journal."

"I'll let all of you go once you give me the password."

"You'll forgive me if I don't believe a word you say," Samantha retorted smartly. But her sarcasm didn't go without a price. The guard instantly slapped her across the face, stinging her cheek, rattling her senses and leaving her dizzy and disoriented. She heard Sean's muffled protest and from the corner of her eye saw him wrestle with his bonds in order to come to her rescue. His attempt to help her was met by a boot plunged to his rib cage. He moaned in anguish and fell over; his head slumped against her shoulder.

"Look," Geoffrey rose from his seat at the computer and stood in front of her. He pointed his pistol at Sean, attached a silencer and cocked the trigger, "Either give me the password or I'll shoot him now."

"MST2k1c" Samantha replied, closing her eyes, and hoping Officer Evans came to their rescue sooner rather than later.

Geoffrey went back to the computer and typed in the password she'd given him. He smiled as the file came up, but as he scanned through the document, his expression grew angry. He rose to his feet, lifted a briefcase from the floor and put the memory stick and the journal inside. He snapped the briefcase closed, then stood there facing the three of them.

Slowly he lifted the weapon from the table and pointed it at Samantha. "I should have known better than to ever trust a woman again. After my own wife turned on me, I never should have let Marjorie into my life. It's a shame I had to kill her, but I see now that she deserved it even more than I thought she did." He stepped closer, aiming the weapon at Samantha's chest. "And you're no less deserving of death yourself," he growled.

He cocked the trigger and Samantha felt Sean lunge over in front of her, trying to block the bullet with his own body. A shot fired, loud and echoing through the chamber. Samantha closed her eyes expecting to feel herself shot. When she didn't, she looked down at Sean assuming he'd taken the bullet for her. But he appeared to be unharmed. Her eyes darted up to find Geoffrey Nielson's body crumpled to the floor in front of her. A burst of gunfire followed and Geoffrey's two goons lifted their arms as David Evans and a complete SWAT team spilled into the chamber.

While David checked Geoffrey's pulse, two officers apprehended Geoffrey's henchmen. Another untied Samantha, Sean and Paul.

"Is Paul okay? He's been out the entire time," Sean asked as soon as the gag was off his mouth.

"His pulse is a little weak, but he should be fine," the officer replied with one hand to Paul's neck. "Bring in the medics. We're going to need three stretchers," the officer spoke into his radio.

Once Samantha was free of her bonds she tenderly put her hand to Sean's cheek, "Are you . . . are you in a lot of pain?"

"I'll be okay," Sean struggled to his feet. Samantha reached out to assist him when he teetered.

"He needs a stretcher," Samantha told the officer.

The man motioned for the paramedics, "Put these two men on stretchers and come back for Nielson. He's dead." The officer turned and addressed Samantha, "What about you, miss? Are you injured?"

"No, I'm fine. I can walk. As the paramedics carried Sean and Paul out of the bunker, Samantha took a moment to look down at Geoffrey Nielson's body. Even though the men had told her he was dead, she wanted to be sure for herself. Squatting down, she put her hand to his neck and felt for a pulse. She wanted to lash out at him, beat upon his chest, scream at him, make him pay for what he had done to her mother, to her family, but he was already dead. Nothing more could be done to him. It hardly seemed like enough. She'd have to leave the rest to God, or in Geoffrey Nielson's case, the buffetings of Satan.

David Evans stood over her. "Miss Reynolds, are you ready to go?" he inquired softly, putting a hand on her shoulder.

She nodded that she was and let him help her to her feet. He put his hand to the center of her back and escorted her out of the dark bunker into the light of a sunny morning.

"I want to ride with Sean to the hospital," she said as they reached the waiting ambulance in the parking lot.

"You can meet him at the hospital," a blonde paramedic retorted.

"I'm going with him," she insisted and looked to David for support.

"Let her go. That's the least we can do for her," David ordered and helped Samantha into the back of the ambulance with Sean and Paul. A paramedic sat between them, dressing Paul's wounds first and attaching an IV. Samantha sat beside Sean's stretcher and held his hand all the way to the hospital.

When they arrived at the hospital, the paramedics removed Paul first. Samantha hovered beside Sean, holding his hand and looking into his eyes.

"I love you, Sam," he whispered. "I've always loved you."

She leaned over and pressed a tender kiss to his bruised lips, "I love you too."

"We're ready to take him inside," the paramedic told Samantha, and she moved aside letting them remove him from the ambulance. She followed as closely as she could until his gurney disappeared behind the emergency room doors.

~ ✧ ~

Samantha stepped outside the hospital and punched a

button on her cell phone, "Travis? You're never going to believe what I have to tell you . . ."

Epilogue

~ ✧ ~

Samantha and Travis stood inside their mother's bedroom, where all of her clothes were boxed up in the center of the room.

"Travis, if you and Sean will load the boxes into the van, I'll run it to Goodwill," Leslie offered as she entered the room and began taping up the boxes.

Travis grabbed the first box after Leslie finished closing it and carried it down the hallway. Just as she taped another one, Sean entered and put his arms around Samantha's waist from behind.

"How you holdin' up, sweetheart?" he asked as he kissed her cheek.

"I'm okay," she caressed his arm that encircled her.

He turned her to face him, "Are you sure?"

"Yeah, I'm fine," she smiled up into his blue eyes.

"Good," he leaned over and gave her a quick kiss on the lips. Then he released her and took the box from Leslie. He carried it out of the room and down the stairs.

"You and Sean seem to be enjoying married life," Leslie smiled at her sister-in-law.

Samantha's broad grin was her only answer.

"I figured a year into this marriage, you two would have

snapped out of the honeymoon stage by now," Leslie winked.

"Yeah, well, Sean is wonderful. I'm crazier about him every day that passes."

"You two should have gotten together years earlier."

"No, I think it was perfect the way it turned out," Samantha replied, holding a bulging box closed so Leslie could tape it shut.

"Really? Why?" Leslie stretched the tape across the top of the box.

"I don't think we would have appreciated what we had if we hadn't both endured some bad relationships first. We might have thought the grass was greener and done something stupid like thrown it all away. But the way it turned out, we're both mature and know what a miracle our marriage is."

"That's a good way to think of it," Leslie stretched another piece of tape across the box.

Travis and Sean reentered the room, took a couple more boxes and left.

"Oh, guess who I saw the other day." Leslie said. "You're never gonna guess."

"Who?"

"Lance Nielson," Leslie answered.

"Poor, Lance. How is he? I felt so sorry for him after the rude awakening he had about his father. Just imagine what it would be like knowing that your own father not only killed his business partner and shoved his body overboard into the ocean, but also killed his girlfriend and his own wife—Lance's mother!"

"I know! I just can't imagine how hard that would be. But he appears to be doing fine. After the liquidation of his father's assets, he ended up having enough left to start his own construction business. It's going very well for him. He said to tell you 'Hi.'"

"Really? I figured he probably hates me."

"No, he said he just feels bad for what you and Sean went through and told me he hopes you have a wonderful life together."

"He's a good guy."

"Who's a good guy?" Sean queried as he entered the room.

"Lance Nielson, I bumped into him the other day, and he told me to tell you both that he wished you the best."

"Oh, well, that's nice of him, especially after everything that's happened," Sean commented.

"Yeah, I thought so too," Samantha replied. "Well, these boxes are ready to go, and I think this is the last of it."

Sean and Travis carried the remaining boxes to the van and shut the door.

"I'm glad you finally got her to clean out Mom's old room. It's time you two settled into the house as your own," Travis put a hand on his brother-in-law's shoulder.

"Yeah, it's been hard for Sam, losing Marjorie like that. But, I think she's finally come to terms with it."

"She's lucky to have someone as patient as you. Most men would be aggravated to use that tiny room of Sam's when there's a perfectly good master bedroom in the house."

"Oh, that hasn't bothered me a bit. I'd be crazy to complain of being too close to Sam," he winked.

Travis laughed, "Hey, that's my sister, you're talkin' about."

"Don't tell her I told you, because she wanted to be the first, but all that closeness has paid off. We're expecting in December."

"Really? No way!"

"Yep," Sean nodded. "But remember, not a word that I leaked it. She wants to tell you and Leslie over dinner. So don't be saying anything to Leslie, or I'll be sleeping in the garage."

Travis laughed and slapped his brother-in-law's back, "Not a word from me. I'll act completely surprised."

Sean and Travis went back upstairs to see if they could help with anything else. Samantha took one look at the Cheshire cat smile on her brother's face and turned to Sean. "You told him, didn't you?"

"What?" Travis pretended to be oblivious.

"You told him, didn't you Sean Anthony Cooper?"

"Oh no, she's pulling out the middle name!" Travis teased. "You're in trouble now!"

"Told Travis what?" Leslie asked, her confused expression moving from Sean to Travis and then to Samantha. "What's going on?"

"You know, don't you?" she stared Travis in the eye.

"He didn't have to tell me," Travis teased. "What else would have coaxed you to move into Mom's room other than needing yours for something else?"

"Are you two having a baby?" Leslie's eyes widened in surprise.

"Isn't it great?" Travis chimed in, not waiting for Samantha to reply. "It's due in December."

"You got all that from me moving our stuff into Mom's room?" Samantha raised a doubtful eyebrow at her brother, then started toward her husband. Sean began laughing, turned and took off running into the hall and down the stairs with Samantha chasing after him. He outran her, but she saw him scamper toward the kitchen. When she got there, he was nowhere to be found.

"Sean Anthony Cooper, come out here and take your punishment!" she couldn't help but smile as she said his name in a tone not unlike her mother's reprimanding.

She passed the pantry and just as she did so, Sean stepped out of it, pulled her inside and shut the door. She squealed with surprise.

"Ah, I have ya now!" he teased. "The tables are turned." He pressed his body against hers, moving her backward until her back flushed against a row of shelves at the rear of the pantry. He planted each of his hands firmly on the shelving on either side of her head, blocking her there.

"I can't believe you told him when I wanted it to be a special announcement!" she scolded, but she wasn't as angry as she pretended to be. Her body wasn't cooperating with her mind. It was too busy responding to Sean's nearness and the thrill of being spirited away into a closet alone with him.

"I'm sorry about that. It just came out. I made him promise not to say anything to Leslie," he replied as one of his hands went to her cheek, his fingers disappearing into her blonde locks.

"Well, one thing you evidently need to learn about Travis is that everything he knows shows in his eyes," Samantha chuckled as Sean's lips descended to her throat.

"I'll have to remember that in the future," he whispered into her ear, and then kissed her neck once again.

"You think I'm going to forgive you this easily?" Samantha retorted, trying to muster her former agitation, but it was fast disappearing with Sean's amorous advances.

"By the time I have my way with you," he nibbled her earlobe, "you'll grant me anything I want."

"Oh, well, aren't you the conceited one!"

His lips hovered seductively over hers as his husky voice conveyed his intentions, "Well, let's see if it's conceit or the simple truth." Samantha's heart raced, thrilled by his teasing manner and the fact that she wasn't completely sure whether he would indeed prove his ability to sway her in a pantry of all places!

She knew from experience there was nothing that Sean Cooper's kisses could not make her forget or forgive. He'd healed her heart, helped her through her mother's death and the investigation thereafter. With him next to her every problem that life could throw at her became not only manageable but completely forgotten. With one more kiss, one more caress, one more stroke of his fingers through her hair, Samantha not only forgot that Sean revealed her secret, but also that her brother and sister-in-law were still in the house wondering what had become of them.

About the Author

~ ✧ ~

Marnie L. Pehrson was born and raised in the Chattanooga, Tennessee area. An avid enthusiast of family history, Marnie integrates elements of the places, people and events of her Southern family and heritage into her romance novels. Her life is steeped in Southern history from the little town of Daisy that she grew up in to the 24 acres bordering the famous Chickamauga Battlefield upon which her family resides.

Marnie and her husband Greg are the parents of six children. She is the founder of multi-denominational www.SheLovesGod.com which hosts the annual She Loves God Virtual Women's Conference the 3rd week of October each year. Marnie has served in many capacities within her church in presidencies of the women's and children's organizations, as a seminary teacher and pianist. Service as family history consultant inspired her foray into historical fiction.

Marnie is also an internet developer and consultant who helps talented professionals deliver their message to the online world. You may visit her projects through www.PWGroup.com.

You may also read more of her work at www.MarniePehrson.com and www.CleanRomanceClub.com Marnie welcomes reader comments and may be reached at marnie@marniepehrson.com.

Marnie's Other Books

Fiction

The Patriot Wore Petticoats

Waltzing with the Light

Rebecca's Reveries

Beyond the Waterfall

Hannah's Heart (in Granite's Love Notes Series)

Angel and the Enemy

In Love We Trust / Second Sight

Nonfiction

10 Steps to Fulfilling Your Divine Destiny

Lord, Are You Sure?

You Can't Fly If You're Still Clutching the Dirt

PURCHASED AT PUBLIC SALE
SURPLUS MATERIALS FROM THE SLCLS